The Ghost in You

Also by Katrina Mountfort

The Ghost in You

Katrina Mountfort

Elsewhen Press

The Ghost in You
First published in Great Britain by Elsewhen Press, 2018
An imprint of Alnpete Limited

Elsewhen Press, PO Box 757, Dartford, Kent DA2 7TQ
www.elsewhen.press

British Library Cataloguing in Publication Data.
A catalogue record for this book is available from the British Library.
ISBN 978-1-911409-22-9 Print edition
ISBN 978-1-911409-32-8 eBook edition

Designed and formatted by Elsewhen Press

This book is a work of fiction. All names, characters, places, planes of
existence, and institutions are either a product of the author's fertile
imagination or are used fictitiously. Any resemblance to actual
organisations, afterlife, sites or people (living, dead or in-between) is
purely coincidental.

FOREWORD

29th March 2016

Hello to anyone out there who might be listening. My name's Rowena and today is going to be my last day on earth. No, I'm not about to top myself; I died twenty-one years ago. This is a story about my life as a ghost, and how I plan to end it. So we'll start on the day I died, back in the days of Britpop. Make of it what you will – and it doesn't always make sense – but please don't judge me. If you'd found love after you died, what would you have done?

CHAPTER 1

6th March 1995

If I'd realised that today was my Last Day, I'd have tried to make the best of it: plant a tree, have a meaningful conversation with my loved ones (not that there were many), and all the important stuff you're meant to do. But as it was, I spent it doped up on Lemsip and self-pity. My nose was blocked and my throat full of gunk and razor blades. So much for a romantic end. Even Trevor, my boss had taken pity on me. That was a first.

"Christ, get yourself home. You'll scare off the customers," he said.

I'd have preferred to stay. Truth was, I loved my job. I enjoyed the dusty, calming presence of old books, and the soothing quietness. Even on a Saturday morning, the Charing Cross Road shop was never overrun with customers. After that, the day was about as boring as a wet Saturday with a stinking cold could be. Once I'd staggered back from the supermarket, I handed over the carrier bags.

"Thanks, lovey," Marjorie said. "Did you get the Emva Cream?"

"As if I'd forget – don't want you getting the shakes." I grinned. "They had those chocolate marshmallows on special offer too, so I got you some."

I guess you think it's kind of weird that my sixty year-old landlady was one of my favourite people in the whole world – I was only nineteen – but the friendship might make more sense once you get to know me. For one thing, Marjorie didn't care much about what others thought of her. Her hair was white, but she made up for its lack of colour by wearing insanely clashing bright clothes – today she had mauve trousers and an orange and fuchsia patterned cardigan.

"Aren't you a darling? And now you're going to join me for a drink." Ah, I hadn't realised I'd be expected to drink that gloop – I'd have bought some cider as well – but Marjorie nodded her head in a way that meant she wasn't going to take no for an answer. "I've got exciting news."

"Ooh, what?" I didn't get my hopes up. I loved Marjorie to bits, but her idea of exciting was a BOGOF at the Co-op. At the moment I was doing her shopping because her hip was buggered and she was on the waiting list for a new one. "I wanted you to be the first to know. Sarah's had the baby. I'm a granny!"

"That's great news." I pasted on a smile. Marjorie's daughter was a Grade A bitch. Marjorie had got it in her head that we might be friends – Sarah was only two years older than me – but she'd had taken one look at my face and not even tried to say the right thing.

"Euww, isn't there anyfink they could do – like, plastics surgery or somefink?" She talked like that, honestly. She wasn't what you'd call an intellectual. Not that I was exactly Stephen Hawking, but we still didn't have the slightest thing in common.

"Nothing that'd transform me into Demi Moore." I'd grinned. It had made Sarah so uncomfortable. People like me weren't meant to joke about it; we were meant to look a bit tragic and smile gratefully at any crumb of pity. She'd barely spoken to me since as if, by coming too close, she'd be hit by the ugly stick too. Don't flinch, I'm allowed to make jokes about myself, but others aren't. That's the rule.

"Is it a boy or a girl?" Does it have 666 tattooed on its forehead?

"A boy, seven pounds ten. Oliver James."

"Oliver James?" I nearly spilt my sherry, which might have been a good tactical move. But of all the names Sarah could have chosen, how had she come up with the name of my dream guy? I'd have expected Shane or Darren.

"George would have been pleased," said Marjorie, gazing at a photo of herself and her husband who, six months ago, had died with as little fuss as he'd caused in life by having a heart attack in his sleep. "He wanted it to be a boy."

I raised my glass. "Let's toast them both. George and Oliver."

"George and Oliver," Marjorie said, clinking glasses.

I took a sip, so syrupy I could almost feel the spots popping out on my chin. Marjorie was probably about to become a hands-on granny. Sarah didn't seem likely to win Mother of the Year, judging by Marjorie's thin-lipped comments about the amount of Bacardi and cigarettes she'd guzzled through the pregnancy.

"When are you going to see the baby?" I asked.

"Thought I'd pop into the hospital tomorrow."

"I'll give you a lift. The buses aren't great on Sundays."

"That's sweet of you, but don't you have better things to do? You should be out meeting men."

"Yeah, well I'm having to beat them off with a shitty stick." I ignored Marjorie's tutting and twisted a strand of hair around my finger. Every so often, my conversations with her took this cringeworthy turn. Did she really think it was so easy? It wasn't as if I could walk into a café and order a cappuccino plus a hot guy with blue eyes.

In my mind, it was a different story, of course. I met my imaginary Oliver every single day. He'd appear behind my shoulder at work, flick his fair hair out of his blue eyes, and ask if I had any books on Romantic poets. I'd direct him to the appropriate section and he'd ask if I was free for dinner that evening. He'd collect me after work and we'd go to that new bar near Leicester Square; I'd have a strawberry daiquiri and he'd have a Belgian beer. Then we'd have dinner on Frith Street or Greek Street – we'd spend ages peering into all the funky little restaurants there before deciding which one. The fantasy split in two at this stage, depending on what mood I was in. Some days we'd go clubbing; other days we'd go to a Soho bar but not one with loud music – I wanted to chat. But at some stage we'd dance, and then would come The Kiss.

I shook myself out of the daydream. It'd never happen. I'd been working in that shop for three years, for God's sake. Mr Perfect was taking a hell of a long time in finding me. And the truth was so pathetic, I'm ashamed to admit it. I'd never been to a club, never even danced with anyone. The closest I'd ever been to a kiss was with Jason from Sunlight, last year. But he was two inches shorter than me and just as he leaned in, his head had jerked away and we were both too embarrassed to try again. I'd been let down by his Tourette's – I liked the idea of random swearing – but his was more a sort of facial gymnastics that freaked me out. After that, he hooked up with little Siobhan, who even managed to look cute in the middle of a grand mal seizure.

"You're doing it again", said Marjorie. "You can't spend your whole life with your head in the clouds. And don't look at me like that. You know I love you coming round here – don't know what I'd have done without you these past months. George was right; I should have learned to drive when I was younger. Too bloody late now. But ... oh, why don't you make the most of yourself, darling? You never ordered that special foundation, did you?"

"Foundation? It's polyfilla I need. And before you start on sunglasses, I struggle to see enough as it is. And that's before we get started on my wonky mouth."

"It's not just that. That jumper hangs on you like a sack. You've got a lovely figure, why not show it off? There are other colours than black, you know. And the way you always have your arms folded – that puts men off too, you know."

I folded my arms more tightly.

But Marjorie hadn't finished. "I don't mean to nag, lovey, but I look at my Sarah – and I want you to be as happy as she is."

Marjorie had a funny idea of happy. All I ever saw Sarah doing was bitching and complaining.

"What does it matter what I wear? You've forgotten one teeny-weeny detail. Once men see my face, they don't look any further south. Oh, don't look at me like that. I'm OK with it; why can't you be? My life's good. I've got loads of friends at Sunlight. Okay, I admit, I'm not doing anything this weekend. But I can't see my best friend because she's got no immune system and I'm a snotty mess of germs. I know you mean well, but I don't need your pity."

"That place is good for you, but I wish we could find you friends somewhere else."

"Why, are you saying the Sunlight kids aren't good enough? That's not very politically correct. You were the one who suggested that I hang out with other disabled kids in the first place. Besides, I go out with the guys in the shop. And there's Marion, my best friend from back home." I felt my jaw tighten. Maybe I shouldn't have mentioned Marion.

"That's the one who got married last year? When did you last see her?"

"Well, she's got a lot on at the moment, but she says I've got to come and stay for the weekend when she's finished the decorating," I felt the heat in my left cheek. Marion had scrawled the note in her Christmas card, three months ago. I wouldn't have minded staying in Marion's tatty spare room, but I wasn't going to beg. Marion had bagged her man. No room in her life for single friends any more, I guess.

Luckily Marjorie decided to give me a break, and we lapsed back to chatting about the new baby. After a second drink – sherry definitely got better the more you had – and every gross detail of Sarah's labour, I spent the afternoon with Rosamunde Pilcher. Trevor had thrown *The Shell Seekers* towards me this morning.

"This looks like the sort of pap you'll lap up," he'd said. "I got some decent stuff this morning but it'd be wasted on you."

"Cheers, Trev," I'd replied with a suitable hand gesture. "And when you've taken your reading snob head out of your arse, you should rehydrate that desiccated heart of yours."

We always spoke to each other like this. I did read so-called literary fiction sometimes, but other times it was just too much of an effort. It'd be years yet before I could afford to go to university. Besides, nothing transported me outside the ordinary in the way romance novels did. Who wanted to read about the bleak and the ugly? I wanted heroines who'd become friends, heroes who'd become lovers. I guess I was a softy at heart.

When I'd had enough of reading, I called Kirsty. "Hey, what are you up to?" I said.

"Cyclops! Thank God you rang! I'm having the weekend from hell. Mum's convinced she's coming down with something, so I'm stuck in my room with only Johnny Depp for company." Kirsty was sixteen, had aplastic anaemia and was waiting for a bone marrow transplant. The drugs that were keeping her alive gave her no immunity, so she was home schooled, which drove her mad. Her mum had taken her to the Sunlight centre last year to 'help boost her social life'. I'd noticed her straight away – hard not to. Her mouth and nose were covered by a huge white mask on which she'd drawn a pair of blood red, pouting lips. She'd taken one look at the group, turned to her mum and muttered, "For God's sake, Mum, I'm dying, not deformed." Luckily, I'd been the only one to hear it and had burst out laughing. We'd been friends ever since.

"Could be worse." I said. "Which one are you watching now?"

"*Edward Scissorhands*."

"Hold me," I said in my best Winona voice.

"I can't," Kirsty nailed Edward's tragic tone. "You know, Ro, I'm thinking of calling that Make-a-Wish foundation and telling them I don't want to die a virgin, so they need to send me a man right now, preferably Johnny Depp. What do you think?"

"It's not a bad idea. Get them to send one for me too; at this rate I'm going to make it to twenty without getting my cherry popped." I hated it when Kirsty joked about dying, but none of her family was a bone marrow match for her and if they didn't find one soon, her chances weren't good. I could never have imagined that I'd have beaten her to it.

"What are you up to?" she said.

"Reading, just for a change. I did a few hours at the shop this morning and had an hour with Marjorie – the bitch troll from hell's had her baby."

"So the spawn of Satan's arrived – poor bugger." Kirsty had never met Sarah but when you had circles of friends as limited as ours, you tended to share a lot of stories.

"Probably –" I broke off at the sound of an almighty crash next door. "Sorry, I just heard a noise from Marjorie's house. I'd better make sure she's OK"

"OK, call me later."

I left the house and shivered – what a foul night. I knocked on Marjorie's door. No reply. She never went out on a Saturday night. Oh no, maybe she'd fallen or worse – or perhaps there was someone in there? I heard a scream. Then silence. Should I let myself in with my spare key, or phone for an ambulance? Police maybe? But there was no sign of forced entry. I returned to my flat and looked out of the back window. Had someone come in through the back garden? It was too dark to tell. My finger hovered over the 9 on my mobile. Then I jabbed it three times before I had chance to dither any more. They told me to wait for the emergency services to arrive.

I waited.

Five minutes passed and I heard nothing from next door. My stomach tied itself into knots, untied and knotted even tighter. What if Marjorie was unconscious? What if I later found out that I could have saved her if I'd got to her sooner? How could I live with myself, knowing I'd done nothing? Surely I should at least place her into the recovery position? That's the trouble with reading so many books – my imagination had devised a million horror scenarios.

It was no good, I couldn't wait any longer.

I took the spare key and paced outside the front door. The person I loved more than anyone in the world – with a guilty pang I admitted, even more than my Dad – might be in danger. And I was doing nothing about it. Before I lost my nerve, I barged in. The first thing I saw was a standard lamp overturned in the hall. Oh hell, my worst fears were confirmed. I picked up a vase, the nearest heavy object at hand. If I could take the intruder unawares, I could hit him over the head. Don't make a sound, Rowena. I tiptoed into the living room. Empty. Where was Marjorie?

I checked each room in turn. No-one downstairs. Then I heard something – footsteps coming from Marjorie's bedroom. I needed to cough. No, hold it, for God's sake! I crept up the stairs. I'd nearly made it to the top. Then I heard the sirens. And before I had time to react, two men shot out from Marjorie's bedroom. Both had black woollen hats jammed down over their heads, and looked as mean as hell. The sort of guys you'd be frightened to bump into on the street, let alone here. What the hell had I done?

"Fuck! Let's get out of here," one said.

There was nowhere I could go. Best run for it.

But the men beat me to it.

"Out of the way, bitch."

One of them pushed me. I fell forwards.

And landed.

I heard the crack, but felt nothing. Why didn't it hurt? But – what the hell? – I couldn't feel anything. I couldn't move my arms or legs.

And then my chest got tight. Breathe, Rowena!

I couldn't. All I could manage was a gasp.

Got to breathe!

I'm going to die!

And the strangest thing – two words repeating in my head, over and over.

Oliver James. Oliver James

Then nothing.

When I came to, I smiled. Thank God, it was just a panic attack. I turned my head – I was lying at the bottom of the steps. Strange, the fall didn't appear to have hurt me at all. Was it the adrenaline? That numbed pain, didn't it? Or nerve damage? Maybe I shouldn't have moved. Think, Rowena, think – what do they do in *Casualty*? I might need a neck brace. I put my hand behind my head and rubbed it. No, there wasn't the slightest ache. I must have got away with it – fallen the right way or something.

I looked around. How long had I been unconscious? The front door was still open. Only minutes, then. I sat up slowly – so far, so good. I eased myself to my feet. Then I heard a muffled cry. Marjorie was still up there! I ran upstairs, two steps at a time. And there she was, wriggling on the bed, a purple scarf stuffed in her mouth, her hands tied up behind her back. What the hell had happened to the emergency services? Her jewellery box was upturned on the bed, cheap strings of gaudy beads lying all over the duvet.

"Marjorie!" I shouted. Weird. My throat didn't hurt. In fact, I didn't even appear to have a cold any more. Adrenaline must be good stuff.

No reply. In fact she didn't register my presence at all. Had the burglars drugged her?

At that point I heard voices downstairs. The police!

"Up here," I shouted but no-one responded.

I ran to the top of the stairs and couldn't believe what I was seeing. No way. What was this – a dream? Two paramedics were doing something with what looked like a CPR machine next to a body at the foot of the stairs – and that body looked like me. I closed my eye, but when I opened it nothing had changed. Except – oh my God, why didn't I notice before? – I had more peripheral vision than usual. My hand flew to the socket – no longer empty! I covered my left eye – I could see through the right one! I blinked. Weird. I felt my forehead and cheek. No scars. Huh? I made my way down the stairs, then stopped, rooted to the spot watching the paramedics try to resuscitate the body. It looked like me, but how could it be? Then one shook his head.

"Looks like spinal shock," he said. "She must be the girl who phoned. They told her to wait, but they all know better, don't they? Have to play the hero."

And then I got it. No. NO! NO!

"No-one down here. The old lady must be upstairs," said a policewoman. Together with a male colleague, she climbed the steps and, when she reached me, walked straight through me. I felt queasy. This wasn't possible. It was delayed shock, surely? An out of body experience?

The female paramedic shivered.

"Did you feel that?" she said to her colleague.

"What?"

"Dunno, I just came over all chilly."

"You're imagining it; it's like an oven in here."

I reached the bottom of the stairs and knelt over my body. I tried to touch my scars, but my hand disappeared into the flesh, as if my fingers weren't real. Come on, Rowena, wake up. This only happens in films. I twisted a strand of my hair, then felt the rough wool of my sweater. Huh, they seemed real. The floor beneath me appeared to be solid under my feet. So it had to be a dream. This didn't make sense at all.

Deep breaths. Stay calm.

But I can't feel my breathing!

I slumped onto the steps and pressed my hands to my head as if the action would fix the idea in my mind. The words of the police floated down from the bedroom.

"... must have broken her neck. She would have died instantly."

"No, not Rowena!" Marjorie's sobs shook the house.

Died.

This wasn't a dream.

I was dead.

And then the pain came, like my stomach was rising, stuffing itself into my throat. How could I feel this intensely, if I was dead? And with the pain came the anger, red hot. This wasn't fair! I couldn't be dead at nineteen! I tried to take hold of my body, to shake it into life, but every time, my hand sank into the body that was no longer me. I screamed and screamed – I just couldn't stop. Oh, what was the point? No-one could hear me.

And then I started crying, but not the snot-and tears sort of crying – my ghostly self didn't produce fluid. But even so, it felt like I was drowning, knocked off my feet by a giant, overwhelming wave of sorrow and gloom. Think what I'd miss. I'd never swim with dolphins, jump out of a plane with a parachute, or drink cocktails on an exotic beach under the shade of a palm tree. Huh, who was I kidding? I'd never have done those things if I'd lived – they were the things that beautiful people did. And do you know the worst thing of all? I'd died without ever being kissed.

CHAPTER 2

6th March 1995

Funny, the things that pass through your mind when you're in blind panic. I glanced at my watch and realised that I was missing *Casualty*. Why was I bothered? I had my own real-life hospital drama, right here. Every time I told myself that it was just a nightmare and that I'd wake up in a minute, something happened to make it more real. The paramedics covered my body. Endless comings and goings. I could see it all, hear it all, but was unable to touch the body. A police officer arrived. Then a doctor – what was he doing? Ah, he had to certify my death. That wasn't the sort of detail you got in dreams. Marjorie was drinking tea. At least the burglars hadn't hurt her, by the look of it, but she couldn't stop crying.

I didn't want to cry any more. I wanted to scream at the whole bloody unfairness of this.

"What are you playing at, God?" I shouted. "Give me a break, just for once. I was trying to do a good thing. So is this my reward? Where's the justice?"

"Do you know who her next of kin is?" the police officer asked.

"That'll be her father; her mother died when she was sixteen." Marjorie shook her head. "He's in Suffolk, but they weren't particularly close. She hardly ever sees him."

Dad. Someone would have to tell him that I was dead. Would he cry for me? In those awful years when Mum was ill, I'd been an inconvenience. The only thing I was good for was doing the cooking – Mum had never been much cop in the kitchen and I'd been making dinners since I was twelve years old. Social services would've had a field day if they'd found out about the accident. But even that had paled into insignificance because of the bigger tragedy it uncovered.

What did I have to do to get attention in that family? It was during the month I'd spent in the burns unit that Mum had finally agreed to see the doctor about the bouts of odd behaviour that we'd all being trying to ignore for months. They discovered her tumour on the day I returned home. The words of comfort were all for Mum, not me.

And then there was just Dad and me.

Dad seemed to resent me being around even more, after that. It was Marjorie, whom I'd met at the funeral, that suggested I come and live in London, in one of the bedsits she and her husband rented out. Marjorie and Mum had been best friends when they were trainee nurses together. It was an incredibly kind gesture – I guess Marjorie just felt sorry for me. Dad had taken the news with his usual air of mild regret, but I saw the relief too. The final child, the afterthought, was off his hands. My two brothers and sister had married and moved out years ago. Apart from a couple of friends who'd stuck by me after the accident, I wouldn't miss anyone. My sister was twenty years older than me, the youngest brother thirteen years older, so we'd never been what you'd call close.

The day I moved to London was the most exciting of my life. It was meant to be my big adventure, you see, the place where all my fantasies would come true. Marjorie's friend even got me the job in the bookshop. I'd work there and go to night school, retake my GCSEs and maybe get to university. And even if my dreams didn't come true, I could more easily blend into the crowds in a big city. Not like Warburton-on-sea, where everyone remembered me before the accident, where I was poor Rowena who used to be such a pretty little thing. I couldn't get away quick enough, only going back at Christmas and on Dad's birthdays. I know that makes me sound like kind of a bitch, but I did try at first. Dad wasn't much of a conversationalist at the best of times though, and my brothers and sister all had their own families by then. When Freddie, my nephew, said, "What's wrong with Auntie Ro's face?" you could have sliced right through the embarrassment in the room. I told him, but my sister told me to shut up; I was scaring him.

So much for my nearest and dearest.

I found a new family in Marjorie and George, and the Sunshine kids. And even though my dream life wasn't coming together as quickly as I'd hoped, I'd made plenty of friends who didn't judge me on my looks and kept my optimism in the city of possibilities.

What was I doing, looking back at my life? The panic bubbled up again.

"This can't be it!" I yelled.

Couldn't anyone hear me?

What now?

I looked at my hands. They seemed solid. I squeezed one against the other and felt a pressure. That was something, I guess.

"Her life had barely begun." Marjorie said, and that set me off again. I cried for what seemed like forever. I'm not sure how long I was there, but I reached the stage where I couldn't cry any more and the house was empty. I raised my eyes to the ceiling, expecting a great voice to boom down from the heavens. This wasn't how I'd expected death to be. None of that life-flashing-before-my-eyes stuff. No tunnels or bright lights. And what came next? As a kid I'd believed in heaven and hell. Father Mitchell's descriptions of years in purgatory used to scare the crap out of me. Was this purgatory? Where were God and the pearly gates and all that?

But there was no sign of God, or anyone else, come to that.

How long would I be here?

I waited.

"So what, I'm a ghost?" I shouted.

No answer.

What did ghosts do, anyway? Think *Ghost*. Think Patrick Swayze!

I guess I must be able to walk through solid objects. Quickly or slowly? I ran to the door, approaching it side-on. Ouch. I'm sure that worked for Patrick. I rubbed my shoulder. More tentatively, I touched the door with my fingers. Oh my God, they disappeared into the wood! Ah, hands first – that must be it. I inched forwards, all of me passing into the wood. It was an odd sensation, a bit like putting your hand into water. No, thicker than water, golden syrup, perhaps. Then I emerged on the outside. I braced myself for the chill of the damp air but felt no difference in temperature. Huh? I looked down at my clothes and grinned. Typical. I was doomed to spend eternity in a purple baggy sweater, black leggings and cowprint furry slippers.

Muswell Hill Broadway was no different to how it was on any other Saturday night, the road shimmering in the wide-eyed glare of headlamps. I heard fragments of conversations, splinters of sounds of people out for a good time, but not lingering outside pubs, their step purposeful, trying not to get drenched. Were all of them alive, or were the streets haunted by others like me?

"Can anyone hear me?" I shouted.

But no-one turned their head.

Guess not.

I walked into the colossal church that was now O'Neill's bar. I'd been here only once before, with Steph, the girl in the downstairs flat with the achingly trendy Rachel-from-*Friends* haircut. Within minutes of arriving, I'd realised that Steph and I weren't kindred spirits. I'd felt out of it; her friends tried and failed to pretend they hadn't noticed my face. Why didn't they come right out and ask me about it? But no, deformity was one of those things, like cancer, to be whispered about, not referred to directly. I'd longed for invisibility that night. Now I'd got my wish.

"Aren't there any ghosts in here?" I shouted louder this time.

Nothing.

Surely I couldn't be the only ghost in London?

Leaving the bar, I groaned. The rain had got worse. But after a few minutes I realised that I wasn't wet. In fact, I couldn't feel the raindrops hitting my skin. A car driving too close to the kerb sent a spray of water over my feet. Instinctively, I jumped away, but my feet stayed dry. Huh, the afterlife had some advantages.

What other senses had I lost? I could hear and see everything around me. In fact, these senses seemed heightened. I heard the click of heels as a group of girls around my age passed by. Their loud cackling felt as if it were directed at me, as if mocking everything I'd never experience.

"How come you get to live and I don't? It's not bloody fair!" I shouted. At least I could still hear my own voice.

I stamped my feet on the ground. They made no sound, but the pavement felt solid.

Could I smell anything? I crossed the road to my favourite fish and chip shop, looking forward to the comforting aroma. But I walked inside and felt nothing. Not the warmth coming from the cabinet that topped the counter, nor the smell of hot oil and vinegar. I needed to make sense of this. What other ghost stories had I read or seen? Ah, yes – *Beetlejuice*. The deceased couple found a handbook to ease their transition. Where was mine? Where would other ghosts hang out?

And then I had it. One of my favourite places in London – Highgate Cemetery. Call me morbid, but I'd always loved hanging out in cemeteries. To me they were places of love. There was evidence of devotion in every gravestone and mausoleum. Beloved wife. Beloved mother. Eternal reminders that these people had made a difference to others, that they'd made their mark on the world.

I quickened my pace and found I could do this effortlessly. Wow, I could even run without getting tired or breathless. And I was accelerating by the second. It was as if my feet didn't quite touch the ground, like the Road Runner cartoons I watched as a kid. Within minutes I'd reached the cemetery gates.

I passed through the wrought iron gates, shivering at the stone and granite shapes that lurked in the gloom. At least, it felt like I shivered. My skin had no goosebumps. Away from the relentless drone of traffic, the silence was absolute and the cemetery creepier than I'd expected. I slowed my pace. I looked at the inscriptions, some flowery, some matter-of-fact, and calculated the span of the lives they commemorated. Age 73, age 86. Lucky them. How was it that despite the dark, I could see everything in such detail? But the night-time world was a cheerless place, all miserable shades of grey. I plunged into the labyrinth of statues and tombs, eyes darting from one side to another, not feeling the cling of wet grass and beaded cobwebs.

"Is there anyone there?" I shouted.

I got my answer soon enough.

A man dressed in motorcycle leathers sat up from behind a headstone. I screamed. Half of his face was grotesquely mutilated, what was left of his cheek blackened with dried blood. He shook his fist at me.

"Shut the fuck up, bitch," he growled.

Then I noticed a woman, so thin she was almost a skeleton, her hair lank, mousy strings. She, too, was sitting by a grave.

"Get out and leave us in peace," she hissed at me. "What the hell do you think you're playing at, coming here?" Before I could answer, she lay down and appeared to fall asleep.

I shrank into the shadows and slumped to the grass. My hands were shaking and the most awful feeling of loneliness came over me. This was the stuff of horror films. If ghosts were so mean to other ghosts, what was I supposed to do for eternity? Surely I couldn't walk the streets alone, never seeing anyone? I'd go mad! I had to end this, now!

But how do you kill a ghost?

In retrospect, my idea wasn't the best, but you have to remember I was still in shock. Near to Archway was a 40-foot bridge over a major road; everybody called it 'suicide bridge' for obvious reasons. I started to run and soon I'd reached the railings. Tricky to climb over; could I pass through them? I pressed my hand against them; oh, yes. As soon as I was halfway through I lost my balance and started falling.

I was flying! This was the greatest feeling ever!

A searing pain pierced my head. Ugh, I was dizzy, horribly dizzy. I put my hands to my temples. Everything around me tipped and span. Was this it? Was I about to pass over to – well, whatever came next? Everything went black.

***

I opened my eyes and smiled. I was looking at the comforting anaglypta of a familiar living room and there was Marjorie in her lime green cardigan, hunched over on the velour sofa. It was all a dream!

"Marjorie, the strangest thing just happened," I said.

But Marjorie didn't turn around.

Was I still dead? What just happened?

I shuffled over to see what Marjorie was doing. Oh God.

She was mounting a photo in a frame – the one she'd taken of me last year. It was when I was experimenting with a new hairstyle. I'd seen an eighties band called the Human League on the telly and experimented with the asymmetric haircut of the lead singer. I didn't keep it up – it made me look like a tragic retro fashion victim. But worn that way, my hair covered half my face and to look at this photo, my smile evening out my mouth, you wouldn't notice anything wrong with my face. This was the photo of a young woman with long chestnut hair, a large expressive mouth and a hazel eye framed by unusually long, curling lashes. This woman was pretty, beautiful even.

A newspaper lay on the floor. I glanced at it and gasped - the same photo was on the front page.

MUSWELL HILL GIRL KILLED. Rowena Hill, 19, was pushed down the steps when she went to investigate burglars ...

The date was on the paper: March 10th. Four whole days had passed since I was here last! Where had the time gone? I read the article and drew in a breath as I took in the tributes.

"She was like a second daughter to me," said Mrs Marjorie Harris, 60. "I never knew anyone with more sensitivity. The fact that young people like her still existed gave me hope for the world. She was always there to lend a sympathetic ear after my husband died last year, not to mention helping me with odd jobs and the shopping – I'm waiting for a hip replacement and can't get out much at the moment. I don't know what I'm going to do without her."

Trevor had called me the shop's best asset, always reliable and cheerful. Huh, shame he never said it to my face. Raya, the bubbly manager of the Sunlight centre had said that I'd touched the life of every young person that had visited the place. Wow. Plenty of the other kids had said nice things about me. Another assistant called me a bundle of joy. Ugh, is that how I'd be remembered? The sunny, plucky disfigured kid who lit up everyone's day? Normally, such cheesy comments would have me reaching for the sick bucket but today they set me off on another bout of tearless crying.

Marjorie took down an old school photo of Sarah from the wall – the one she hated that was all red hair and freckles – and replaced it with the one of me. Then she set to framing another picture, that of a baby, a beautiful boy with eyes so blue they seemed to leap out of the picture. Funny, I'd never thought much about babies before – I'd assumed I'd probably have them one day but I was never the sort of girl who drooled whenever I saw one. But now I couldn't take my eyes off baby Oliver. Perhaps it was because he reminded me of yet another thing I'd never experience.

Oliver James, Oliver James.

What was it about Sarah's baby that seemed to call out to me? And why had I turned up back here after that horrible encounter in the graveyard? I cast my mind back to Patrick Swayze. His ghost had stayed around for a reason – to avenge his murder. So what was my reason? The burglars were hardly likely to show up here again.

And then I thought of my Kirsty. Her health had been going downhill, and recently her conversations had got more macabre than usual. Maybe I was meant to hang around until she was ready to kick the bucket, too? Yes, that made sense. I left the house, ran to her place, and raised my hands. Ha! Straight through! The passing-through-doors trick was getting easier. Soon I'd made it to her bedroom. She was lying in bed, watching – oh God – *Ghost*. Her eyes were red-rimmed and, judging by the deep black rings under her eyes, she hadn't been sleeping. Even her hair, normally sickeningly gorgeous – long, blonde and glossy – was ratty.

"It's OK, Kirsty, I'm here," I said. "I'll look out for you now."

But she didn't react. Not a peep. I noticed that her face was more puffy than usual.

"Those steroids are a bitch, aren't they?" I spoke louder this time.

No reaction.

"Come on, Kirsty. Surely you can tell I'm here."

I waved my hands in front of her face.

Nothing.

And then I started to feel dizzy again. I looked up to the sky. Come on God, give me a break. Can't I at least spend a bit of time with my best mate? But no, the room was going black … And guess what? I was back in Marjorie's living room.

What the hell?

Was this where I was meant to be? Was I meant to watch over Marjorie? Why? Was this ever going to make sense?

Then I realised that time had passed once more. Marjorie was dressed in a sober black skirt and blouse, not her style at all. The doorbell rang; she heaved a heavy sigh and put on a grey coat. She must have borrowed that from someone – she hated grey. And that's when I got it. She was going to my funeral, and I was meant to go with her. Waiting at the door was Raya and – oh God, a minibus full of Sunlight kids. I followed Marjorie into the bus. And for the whole two-hour journey to Suffolk, I listened to them all talking about me. The only one not speaking was Kirsty, who sat next to Marjorie and whimpered for the whole journey, like an animal caught in a trap.

"What's the point of showing me this?" I shouted to the sky. Sounds stupid, I know, a bit like the way I'm telling this story now, but I had to make myself believe that someone up there was listening. "I can't go back and change anything."

But the real surprise was to come. My parish church back home was one of those gorgeous square-towered East Anglian ones that dominated the landscape for miles around, and it was already half-full when we arrived. I wandered up and down the aisle and saw faces I hadn't seen for years, including Marion, the schoolfriend I thought had forgotten me, but her red eyes and blotchy face told a different story. And every single one of my family was there: my dad, my sister and two brothers, and their kids, all ten of them. The tributes were never-ending. Even Jason from Sunlight got up to make a speech, though his face jerked when he said I was the loveliest girl he'd ever met, probably because Siobhan was shooting him daggers. Shame I had to die to realise how loved I'd been in life.

Then – you guessed it – the dizziness overwhelmed me. Back I went to Marjorie's living room, and she was wearing a short-sleeved, flowered cotton dress and no tights. I guess a few months must have passed.

"So what now?" I said to her.

As if in answer, Marjorie wandered to her shelf of videos and stayed there a while before choosing one.

"This was your favourite, wasn't it, lovey?" Marjorie said to the photo, and slipped the tape into the player.

I smiled as the familiar music struck up.

"Good choice, Marjorie," I said and settled back in the sofa to lose myself in *Now Voyager*. Maybe this wasn't a bad way to spend eternity.

CHAPTER 3

29th March 2014

As usual, I woke up in Marjorie's living room. Over the years, I'd seen no end of changes there. Slim boxes containing discs had replaced her collection of videos. Her TV had become wider and slimmer. The anaglypta remained but was now yellow. There was a new three-piece suite and a growing collection of photos, but my image on the wall had never changed position. I rubbed my eyes: everything around me was monochrome. That was odd; I never materialised at night. I hauled myself up the stairs, feeling sluggish, as if I'd woken from a deep sleep.

I floated through the closed door to Marjorie's bedroom. Oh no! How many years had I skipped this time? Marjorie had shrunk; I swear she seemed about half her usual size. I could see right through her sparse white hair; her face had more lines and less colour. And I didn't like the sound of her breathing – wheezy and uneven. Then I heard a rattle in her throat. Ah, that's why I was here.

I'd heard that rattle once before, just before Kirsty died, almost a year after me. I'd visited her whenever I could but never for long. My trips were usually cut short by the dizziness that sent me back to this room. Until Kirsty got pneumonia. At that point, the strange forces that ruled my existence decided to give me a break and let me stay for the four days it took her to die. It wasn't one of my best memories. But at the same time as my heart was twisting at the sight of my friend struggling for breath, my excitement was spiralling out of control. Surely I'd get to see Kirsty's ghost when she died?

But the end had been a massive anti-climax. Kirsty had risen from her body and her face – pink-cheeked and healthy-looking for the first time in years – broke into a huge grin at the sight of me. But before she'd had time to say anything, I got dizzy and faded away, and when I reappeared in Marjorie's living room, two whole years had passed.

How unfair was that?

I didn't see Kirsty again until even more years had passed, but that's another story.

Now I smiled down at the lady who'd needed me to stay around – at least I assumed that was why I was here. I often seemed to turn up when Marjorie was having some sort of drama. Her old age had been uneventful, a gradual slowing down, like an old clock that needed winding. She hardly ever needed me these days. But the end was coming – I was certain of it. Surely this was the moment I'd been waiting for in – how many years had it been?

"Don't worry, Marjorie; you'll soon be free," I said.

Marjorie inhaled sharply, a loud gulping sound, then breathed out for the last time. I froze in anticipation. Would she see me? Then she sat upright and her mouth lurched into a grin, deepening the crease of her dimples. But where were the rest of her wrinkles? I gasped – she looked so young and her hair was a gorgeous shade of copper. I'd seen a photo of my mum and Marjorie in their early twenties, and that's how she looked now. Except I don't suppose she wore a daffodil yellow nightie in her twenties.

"Hello, lovey," she said.

"Marjorie, at last!" I flung my arms around her and my breath caught in my throat. It had been so long since I'd had physical contact with anyone or anything, I'd almost forgotten what a hug felt like. Her arms held me and it was the best feeling ever. I thought my heart would burst there and then.

It was a long time before either of us was able to speak.

"It's so good to be able to talk to you," I said.

"You too. I guess I finally pegged it," Marjorie said, nodding at her body on the bed.

"Sorry, yeah."

"No need to be sorry, darling. To be honest, I'd had enough. A long life isn't all it's cracked up to be. So what's next? Have you come to guide me into the next life?"

"I don't know. I've been here since I died."

"But that's been – how long is it now – nineteen years?"

"Is it? I'm not sure. You see, whenever I go anywhere, I never stay more than a few hours. And then it's like I get pulled away. I get dizzy then lose consciousness. When I wake up, time's moved on. Sometimes days, sometimes months or years. You – the old you, that is – look older than when I last saw you. I think I've been gone for a few years this time. What year is it?"

"2014. Ooh, that means you've been dead for as long as you were alive." Marjorie's eyebrows drew together. "But I wonder why you didn't pass over?"

"I think perhaps I was meant to wait, that I was looking after you. When I awoke I was nearly always back in your living room."

"You're kidding?"

"Nope. It took me ages to work out why, but I think I must be your guardian angel or something."

"So you were looking out for me all along." Marjorie smiled. "Funny, I've often felt something – guess you'd call it a presence. I used to wonder if I was going barmy."

"No, I've sat beside you, watched films with you, all sorts. Sometimes I'd turn up in places I didn't recognise, as if you had the power to summon me. There was this time outside a supermarket, when two teenage girls were watching you fumbling as you put your change in her purse. I could see them sizing you up. One of them said, "Easy target." So I swung for her. My fist went straight through her, of course, but she definitely felt something – she flinched. Then I thumped the second one. They looked at each other, panic all over their faces, and changed their minds."

"But – no offence, lovey – but why was it you looking after me and not George or, later on, my Sarah? No, don't answer that. You were always more of a daughter to me than she ever was. Perhaps that's it."

"I don't get it either, but you were the person I loved most in the world. Perhaps I chose it."

She leaned over and squeezed my hand. "I'm glad you did. If I could have chosen my guardian angel, you're exactly what I would have wanted. Are there a lot like you, people who've hung around, I mean?"

"I don't know. I met a couple of ghosts in Highgate cemetery, just after I died. Scared me to –" I giggled. "I almost said 'to death'. And then I saw others in cemeteries, but they were all asleep. So I never looked for anyone else. This is the first conversation I've had in years." Well, not quite. Perhaps it was best not to tell Marjorie about Oliver. Not yet, anyway.

"Ooh, you poor thing."

"It was horrible at first. I was so lonely, so frightened. But I adapted. I had no choice. And then I came to realise that I could do whatever I liked. I see new releases at the cinema and go to concerts."

"But all that time on your own …"

"But what was nineteen years for you was – I don't know – probably no more than a year or so for me, because I skipped so much time. I've missed having people to talk to, but otherwise it's not so bad. And there's no-one pointing and staring and wondering what happened to my face."

"Your face. I hadn't even registered. You've got your eye back! You're not scarred any more!"

"That's right. I've no idea why. It's happened to you, too. You look about fifty years younger."

Marjorie patted her skin and gave a little squeal. "Well, how about that? So – huh, this is the oddest conversation I've ever had – what else have you been doing with yourself?"

"I tried going to college, but because I can't control the time I'm around, that didn't work. Sometimes I'd go to pubs and restaurants and eavesdrop on other people's conversations."

"I like the sound of that." Marjorie smiled. "The number of times I've said, 'if only I could be a fly on the wall'."

I grinned. People watching had become a bit of a hobby of mine. I loved observing the way people interacted in groups – who was feeling uncomfortable, who was secretly pissed off with someone else. I learned to recognise when people were lying – a head movement, a tensing of the shoulders. I watched couples on first dates, lapping up every detail, from their body language to the amount of personal information they told each other. In death, I guess you could say I became a student of life. If only I could have my time again, I'd make a better job of it.

"Don't get too excited," I said. "I've got a feeling you won't be hanging around for long."

"Do you think we're going to pass over together?" Marjorie asked. "I'd like that. Just think, George and Sarah will be there waiting for me, and your Mum and Dad, God bless them."

So Dad had died, had he? I suppose he must have, he'd be pushing ninety by now. Did I want to see Mum again? My memories of her had become so tangled up with resentment that it was hard to remember her clearly. Can't say I was keen on seeing vile Sarah again, but I guess I had no choice. Then Marjorie grabbed my hand.

"Oh, lovey! Look, isn't it beautiful?"

"What?"

I couldn't see anything. But Marjorie was staring straight ahead, her face lighting up, with a sort of happiness I'd never seen on anyone – I guess you'd call it bliss. And then Marjorie's hand dissolved under the pressure of mine. And she faded until nothing remained except – was I imagining it? – a kind of glow where her ghost had been. All that was left was the body on the bed. And I was still here!

"What about me?" I shouted.

I stared at the ceiling, overcome with panic.

What sort of sick joke was God playing on me?

Was I doomed to stay here forever?

I sat on the bed, waiting to follow Marjorie, but the door to the other dimension had been slammed in my face for a second time. I lay down. Perhaps if I tried to fall asleep, I'd disappear for a few more years. Perhaps I was meant to stick around until the end of my natural lifespan? That could be forty more years. But what was the point?

Nothing happened. After a few hours I heard the sound of a key in the door downstairs. A voice shouted Marjorie's name. I walked to the landing and saw a chubby, youngish woman in a white-trimmed pink tunic dress and apron. How long had Marjorie needed someone to look after her? She jogged up the stairs and headed for the bedroom, not so much walking as dancing, all the time humming a song I didn't know.

"Rise and shine, Marjorie, it's after nine," she chirruped. Ugh, she was irritatingly chirpy – how did Marjorie stand that every morning? She looked at Marjorie, frowned, put two fingers to her neck and then gave a little gasp and started crying. That was good to see – she genuinely cared for Marjorie. She pulled a flat object from her pocket, put it to her ear and started speaking. I'd seen more and more of these over the past few years – everyone seemed to have them. Mobile phones were way bigger when I was alive and not many people had them.

"Jill? I'm at Marjorie Harris's. Looks like she died in her sleep ... no, I'm OK, honestly. It's just, she was one of my favourites ... Thanks, should I wait until they turn up? ... OK ... No, her daughter died a few years ago. There's a grandson isn't there ... comes to visit? I'll check the notes."

Oh ... of course.

Oliver.

I'd see Oliver again.

"Yes, here it is. Next of kin, Oliver Spencer," said the carer. "There's a number. Should I call?"

At that moment I was glad I hadn't passed over with Marjorie.

Nineteen years – Oliver would be the same age as me! Finally, he was a man: that beautiful boy who had touched my soul – literally – from the first moment I met him.

***

14th March 1995

Oliver had been a baby, the first time I met him. It wasn't long after I died; I'd materialised in the living room feeling annoyed – before that I'd been watching *Four Weddings and a Funeral* with Kirsty and hadn't got to the end – and heard Marjorie telling Sarah and Terry, her husband, all about me.

"Sad, innit?" said Sarah. "Wasn't much of a life." She turned to Terry. "She was two years younger than me. D'you remember her?"

"Yeah, she was at your dad's funeral, wasn't she?" he said. "One eye. Huge lumpy red scar over one side of her face." He scowled. Huh, as if he was such a catch, with his fading tattoos, yellow teeth and eyebrows that formed a single bushy stripe across his forehead.

"Yeah, made me feel sick just to look at her," Sarah ran her hands through her peroxide perm. She turned to Marjorie and scowled. "You went a bit overboard with the journalist, making out she was some sort of saint. How's it make me look? You coulda called me if you needed someone to talk to after Dad died."

"With Rowena, I didn't need to call." Marjorie thinned her lips so much they almost disappeared.

Good for you, Marjorie.

I focussed all my hate on Sarah. Ooh, it'd be good to be able to poke one of her eyes out. She wouldn't be quite so smug then. Marjorie was holding Oliver. At first sight, I have to admit, I was disappointed in him. He was asleep, not even wriggling. Sarah looked down at her flabby stomach.

"I'll be glad when I get my figure back," she said, taking a cigarette packet from her handbag. Jesus, she wasn't going to blow smoke over little Oliver, was she? She probably smoked when she was pregnant too, selfish cow. Why had she put herself out by having a baby? I guess Oliver was the result of an accident, like I'd been.

"Not in front of Oliver!" Marjorie said. "Besides, aren't you breastfeeding?"

"Hell, no," said Sarah, smoothing down her way-too-tight top to expose a huge expanse of cleavage. Another reason to hate her. I hadn't exactly been flat up top, but I'd always longed for big boobs. Not that I'd have worn low-cut tops like that, even if I had been well endowed. "Don't want these going saggy, do we?"

"Too right," Terry leered at Sarah's boobs.

"Fucking creep," I said.

Poor Oliver – tattooed Terry looked about as promising a dad as Sarah did a mum. Then I heard a sound from the bundle in Marjorie's arms – I swear it was a giggle.

"Come on, Oliver, how about a smile for your Nan?" Marjorie said, with that simpering voice people always put on for babies. Why? Surely they'd rather be spoken to like humans, not pets?

I moved closer to get a good look at him. Wow. His eyes

were even bluer than in the photo – like a swimming pool – and blond eyelashes. And once more I got that feeling, that Oliver was important to me.

"Oliver, you're beautiful, aren't you?" I said.

And then he looked directly at me and smiled. No, he couldn't have, surely? Was it coincidence? Or wind?

"That's better," Marjorie said, but Oliver's eyes were fixed on me.

"Can you see me?" I asked.

Oliver chuckled.

"Oh my God. You heard me, didn't you?"

I moved my finger from side to side, and there was no doubt – Oliver's eyes were following its movement! I held my finger to Oliver's hand. His tiny fingers curled around it and grasped it – so firmly that I felt the pressure. And the most incredible feeling passed through me – a thousand tiny bolts of joy. I let out a cry, but the moment didn't last. Marjorie smiled.

"Aw, look. He wants a finger to hold." She put her own finger into Oliver's curled hand, passing right through mine.

"Ooh, I just got that feeling again," said Marjorie. "Like someone walked right over my grave."

Oliver started crying and the moment was gone. But it was only the start …

CHAPTER 4

29th March 2014

"Is that Oliver Spencer?" the carer said into her phone.

Not for the first time, my lack of physical form frustrated me. I should be the one to tell him. But the carer carried on. At least her voice had dropped an octave. This was obviously her 'breaking the news' voice. It was only marginally more sincere than her 'bright and breezy' one.

"I'm afraid I have some bad news about your grandmother. She passed away in her sleep."

A pause.

"Yes, I'm her carer. I found her about five minutes ago. She looks at peace ... yes, you'll have to register the death. You'll need a medical certificate confirming the cause of death first; a doctor's on his way. ... Don't worry, there are leaflets that explain the whole process to you."

Poor Oliver. Hell of a lot for him to cope with on his own. It had been a few years since I'd last seen him – at his mum's funeral. And now he'd be the same age as me! I couldn't get my head around it.

I guess by now you're thinking that my sticking around so long as a ghost had more to do with Oliver than Marjorie. I certainly was; I'd had loads of theories, analysing them and re-analysing until I tied myself in knots. Maybe I was meant to be his guardian angel, not Marjorie's? I'd tested the theory, following him to school when he was being bullied, even going to his house when he was having a rough time with his 'uncles', but each time I'd been pulled back to Marjorie's house. Go figure. All I can say is that watching Oliver grow up had been the best thing that had ever happened to me, in life or death, and when I was around him, I felt more energised, charged even. It made no sense at all; he was just a kid.

Oliver.

Would he even remember me, or had he written me off as a figment of his over-active imagination? The only memorable parts of my ghostly existence had been with him. To tell you all about them, I need to jump through time.

***

4th October 2000

Oliver had his nose in a picture book when I turned up in the room. I smiled at his messy mop of red hair. He'd got that colour from his mother's side, though you'd never know; Sarah's was always dyed yellow-blonde and Marjorie's hair had been white for years. Sarah blew her nose and sniffed.

"I mean, he said it was just a bit of fun, but that's such a bloody cliché, isn't it? Once a cheater always a cheater," she whined, twisting the belt loop of the low-slung jeans that showed off how successfully she'd lost that baby fat.

"Ha, serves you right, cow," I said.

Sarah didn't deserve a man, even a cheating scumbag like Terry. Even though I was never able to stay with Oliver for long, I'd seen enough to know she hadn't improved. The poor kid lived on chicken nuggets, fish fingers, baked beans and cheap burgers. She even left him on his own sometimes; I'd have given anything to be able to call social services.

"He'll come crawling back. He always does." Marjorie rolled her eyes.

"I don't think so this time. He says they're in love." Sarah twisted her wedding ring.

Poor Oliver. Terry hadn't exactly been a positive role model. All he ever did was swig lager out of the can, fart and put sport on the telly when Marjorie was trying to talk. But I guess he was better than no dad at all.

"You deserve better," I said without thinking. Would he hear me? I hadn't tried to speak to him since he was a baby; I didn't want to scare him.

But Oliver turned in his seat to look at me, and didn't seem the least bit scared. He blinked and smiled.

"Hello," he said.

"Who are you talking to?" Sarah snapped

"The nice lady behind the settee," he said.

Sarah and Marjorie turned to follow his gaze, looked at each other and Sarah shrugged.

Still staring at me, Oliver asked, "What's your name?

"Rowena," I said. Not my smartest move, I know, but the novelty of someone speaking to me was so incredible that I spoke without thinking.

"Ro-wee-na." He said the word slowly and deliberately, emphasising every syllable. "That's nice."

"Oh no, not again," said Sarah. "Why did you tell him her name?"

"I didn't." Marjorie frowned.

"Ssh." I put a finger to my mouth.

But Oliver was gazing at me with open mouth, eyes almost popping out of his head, as if his favourite cartoon character had materialised in front of him.

"He must have heard us talking about her," Marjorie continued. "Bright little thing, isn't he?"

"She's there." Oliver pointed at me. "She doesn't want me to tell you, though."

"What does she look like?" Sarah asked.

"She's the prettiest lady I ever saw. She looks like that picture on the wall," – he pointed at the photo of me – "but she hasn't got that silly haircut."

"How many eyes has she got?"

"Two. Don't be silly, Mummy. Everyone's got two."

"Thank God for that. For a minute I thought he really could see her." Sarah's eyes darted to the wall. "You should take down her photo, Mum. I don't like all this ghost business. His teacher says he spends too much time daydreaming and not enough time playing with the other kids."

"That girl sacrificed her life to save me. That picture stays," said Marjorie with an emphatic nod. "So he's got a vivid imagination. I think that's a good thing."

"So do I," I said.

"The teacher mentioned a child psychologist," Sarah said. "He's clever, but way behind on his social development."

I winced. Is that how teachers spoke these days? How could you put a benchmark on social development? Surely each kid developed in his or her own time? Wonder what they'd have made of me, after the accident. Before then, I'd been one of the most popular girls in the class. Afterwards, my friends had dwindled away, partly because of embarrassment, partly a practical move. No boys would approach a group of girls at a disco if one of them only had half a face.

I turned to face Oliver. "Say you want to go to the toilet," I said.

He was a smart little kid, all right. Without giving his bitch mum or Marjorie any sign that he could see me, he did as he was told. Once we were out of the room I patted the stair. He sat down next to me.

"Are you really a ghost?" he whispered.

"Yes, but you're the only person who can see or hear me. I've no idea why; you must be a very special boy. But your mum's going to get mad if you carry on talking to me. If you see me in future, pretend you haven't noticed. It can be our secret. It's nice having secrets, isn't it?"

Oliver nodded and smiled. I wasn't sure whether I should be alarmed or flattered by how completely he seemed to trust me.

"And remember, Oliver. There's nothing wrong with you. Nothing at all."

His smile lit the hallway. And I knew that, from now on, I'd do whatever I could to look after him as well as Marjorie.

*****

29th March 2014

I left the doctor with the body that was no longer Marjorie, and went downstairs to take a look around the room I knew in ridiculous detail, down to the scuffs on the skirting boards and each crack on the ceiling. I guess someone else would be living here soon. Would I still get pulled back here? That would be bizarre – Marjorie had been as much a part of this house as the sagging sofas. Maybe I had a deep connection to the house itself. No, it must be Oliver. Nothing else made sense. Wonder what he looked like these days?

My eyes settled on my favourite picture of Oliver, at Regent's Park zoo. He must've been around eight then. The elephant enclosure was behind him, and I was next to him, but, of course, the camera hadn't picked me up.

"We had fun that weekend, didn't we sweetheart?" I said, reaching to stroke his hair. I shivered – after all this time I still hated it when my fingers passed through solid objects when I didn't want them to. But they hadn't gone through Oliver, that weekend.

***

9th June 2003

Marjorie had been pretty down, that year. She'd had her second hip replaced and it had taken her longer to bounce back than last time. So I'd been on the scene more than usual. We'd been watching *Billy Elliot* when Sarah and Oliver arrived.

"At last," Marjorie said. "You said 5:30."

My heart leapt, but at the same time I moved to hide behind the new green velour curtains. Oliver couldn't be trusted not to give himself away by smiling when he saw me. He was wearing a blue T-shirt with a yellow square cartoon character who was all eyes and goofy grin. Sarah's hair was now straight but still blonde, and her handbag was bigger than her tiny denim miniskirt.

"Sorry, I can't stay, I'm already running late," said Sarah. She took a drag on her cigarette, pulling her lips sideways, "Here's his things. He goes to bed at eight-thirty and no later."

"Don't worry, we'll be fine, won't we, Oliver?" said Marjorie. The last few years had given her an extra padding of flesh but she hadn't toned down her patterned clothes, and she was starting to resemble an overstuffed sofa. The warmth of her smile hadn't faded either, and it was clear that Oliver adored her.

Oliver gave a little nod.

"OK, see you on Sunday night." Sarah tottered off in her white boots, then gave a little squeal. "I still can't believe he's taking me to Paris!"

Neither could I. Sarah seemed to have no trouble finding men but keeping them was a different matter altogether. God knows how she'd managed to screw a weekend break out of the latest guy. I hadn't seen him, but I guess he wasn't good father material either. Poor Oliver's mouth seemed to turn downwards all the time these days. I'd have to have a chat with him as soon as I got the chance. I spoke to him whenever I could, but it didn't seem fair to overdo it. He had it tough enough without me haunting him.

"Now, Oliver, since your mum's having a little holiday, why don't we have one, too?" said Marjorie. "I thought we'd go to Madame Tussaud's tomorrow, then maybe the zoo on Sunday. How does that sound?"

It sounded like heaven. I wish Marjorie had been my mum. My mum and dad were in their fifties when I'd been Oliver's age but they'd seemed even older – as if they'd used up all their parenting skills on my older brothers and sisters and couldn't be bothered making any effort with me. Marjorie, now in her late sixties, was a powerhouse of energy in comparison.

"Brilliant!" said Oliver with a rare smile.

"Now, what time is it, ooh, still more than an hour to teatime," said Marjorie. "Tell you what, I'll put the telly on for you. Do you want a glass of orange and some biscuits?"

"Yes please," said Oliver.

As Marjorie left the room, I sat next to Oliver.

"Hello, Ro-wee-na," said Oliver, a smile spreading over his face. The funny thing about him was that he never seemed surprised to see me, even if it had been months since we last spoke. And I loved the way he said my name. Most of my friends used to call me Ro, and Marjorie had always shortened the first syllable – R'weena. The way Oliver said it, it was beautiful.

"Hello, sweetheart," I said. "Who's that on your T-shirt?"

"SpongeBob Squarepants. He's brill," he said and explained in entertaining detail who the cartoon character was. Then he said, "We're going to the waxworks and the zoo. Do you want to come with us?"

"I'd love to." Could I? I'd never been to either. In fact I'd never been to any zoo – my mum and dad hadn't been into family days out – I guess they had their fill of that with my older siblings. By now I was used to going out of the house to explore London and with immense concentration I could make myself stay around for up to twelve hours – I'd even managed to see the fireworks on the Thames at the turn of the millennium. "Ssh, here's your nan."

Marjorie came in, carrying a glass of orange juice and a plate of biscuits. "There you go." She handed him the glass and set the plate on the table. "There's Jaffa cakes and ginger nuts."

Oliver flinched.

"What is it? Don't you like ginger nuts?" Marjorie asked.

His face flushed crimson, his eyes darting downwards. Ah – ginger nut. Of course. I held his hand.

"Kids at school can be mean," I whispered to him. "Don't listen to them."

"Hey, what's the matter?" Marjorie asked. "You know you can tell your old nan anything."

"That's what they call me at school," Oliver muttered.

"What?" Marjorie opened her mouth and then shut it. "Ah. Have the other kids been picking on you?"

Oliver nodded, his eyes brimming over with tears. Why did this boy get to me so much? I wanted to gather him up in my arms, sit him on my lap and protect him from the world. Luckily, Marjorie did the job for me. I'd never seen Sarah cuddle him, not once.

"Ooh, you are getting to be a big boy, aren't you?" she said. "Have you told your mum about this?"

Oliver shook his head.

"She's always out with Uncle Steve," he said.

"Tell me all about it then."

"It's these lads in my class. They pull my hair …"

And then he was crying, face buried in Marjorie's ample bosom. She patted his head and drew him closer. Weirdly, I still felt all sorts of sensations internally although logic told me that my physical form was no longer a body. Now I felt a clenching in my chest. If I had a heart, this little boy was tearing at it.

"It happened to me, too, when I was at school," Marjorie said. "Your mum too. It was carrot top, in my day."

Oliver looked up and sniffed, wiping his eyes on the back of his hand.

"Take no notice of them," Marjorie continued. "You know what I used to tell the other kids? I'd say they were only jealous because I was more colourful than them. That's when I started wearing bright clothes. Who wants to be one of the crowd? Me, I'd rather stand out."

"That's brilliant!" I said. How did Marjorie always manage to say the right thing?

When Oliver stopped crying, Marjorie left once more for the kitchen to prepare his dinner.

"Don't let those bullies upset you, Oliver," I said. "Remember that you're special. The most special boy in the whole world."

"Why can't you be with me all the time, Rowena?" he asked.

"I wish I could, sweetheart."

"Did you say something, Oliver?" came a voice from the kitchen.

Later that evening, I crept into Oliver's bedroom and gazed at his face, sad even in sleep. Without thinking, I brought my hand to his cheek to move a strand of hair. Incredibly, it moved. I stroked his hair, luxuriating in the feel of those fine silky fibres. Then I leaned over and kissed his forehead. For a moment I was overcome by the familiar dizziness that meant I was on my way back to the living room, but it subsided.

That's when I became certain that I'd been put on this earth to be Oliver's guardian angel. I think I managed to cram a whole year's worth of missed childhood experiences into that weekend. As well as the waxworks and the zoo, we went to a park, fed the ducks and I drooled as he went to McDonald's. Miraculously, I managed to stay with Oliver the whole time. And after that, I tried to go home with him, planning to go to school with him the next day and help him handle the bullies.

Instead, I felt dizzy as soon as I left the house with him and Sarah. I blacked out, woke up in Marjorie's living room a month later, and next time I saw Oliver, it was Christmas.

So that blew the guardian angel theory out of the water.

What the hell was I here for?

CHAPTER 5

29th March 2014

Lucky Marjorie to have made an early exit – the rituals of death weren't exactly worth sticking around for. The paramedics hauled her body onto a stretcher, covering her with a sheet as if the appearance of a dead body was offensive. I looked at her face for the last time, but already it seemed different. What remained of Marjorie was only a shell; her transition to whatever came next must have been complete. But part of me was pleased I hadn't gone with her. I had to admit, I couldn't wait to see how Oliver had turned out.

So what now? When would Oliver arrive? I looked at a photo of him as a teenager. Adolescence hadn't been much kinder to Oliver than it had to me. Instead of scar tissue, he'd had to cope with the march of freckles and acne across his perfect skin. He rarely looked for me in those days, too wrapped up in reading or some sort of handheld electronic game. I'd spent hours watching over his shoulder but I couldn't see why he was so obsessed with it – it made me dizzy.

Watching Oliver became my way of measuring time, and when he was around eleven to fourteen, it started to accelerate. I skipped the year 2007 entirely. I told you my existence didn't always make sense. And then, around five years ago, came shocking news. It started with Sarah in tears over her latest crap relationship. Her hair was so long at that stage it came halfway down her back – I discovered she'd had extensions in it – and she'd put on weight, but she still wore jeans that barely skimmed her hips. These days, a roll of flesh hung over them.

"How didn't I see it coming? I really thought Rob was

different," she said between sobs.

"You said that about Graham." Marjorie's voice was suitably acidic. "I did tell you it was hasty to invite Rob to move in." Her voice softened. "Come on love, you've survived worse than him. Anyway, what about this fantastic school report of Oliver's? Nice to think someone in the family's got some brains."

But Sarah sniffed. "Huh, he keeps them well-hidden."

That was pretty shitty even by her low standards. Over the years I'd discovered that Oliver was so brainy he'd skipped a grade and was the youngest in his class. I slapped Sarah's face. By now I'd discovered that if I was angry enough, people felt it. She flinched but Oliver didn't react. Perhaps he could no longer see me?

The weird thing about watching Sarah get older, was knowing that I'd be almost the same age if I'd lived. When Sarah smiled, which wasn't often, lines formed at the corners of her eyes. She also had lines running up and down around her lips, hardly surprising I guess, since she'd had them wrapped around a cigarette for most of her life. I'd be in my mid-thirties; it didn't seem that old. Would life have ground me down as much as it had Sarah? Marjorie aged much better apart from the fact that her knee was now buggered and about to be replaced.

Oliver flushed, put down the book he'd been reading, muttered something unintelligible. His voice had deepened such a lot recently, yet another reminder that he was no longer the sweet little boy I cared for so much. Then he slunk out of the room. He wore awful clothes these days – baggy jeans that seemed too big for him, showing the top of his boxer shorts, and a top with a hood. As he left, I couldn't resist emerging from behind the armchair, smiling and winking at him. He saw me that time – I was sure of it – but he didn't smile. So I followed him to the foot of the stairs.

"Being a teenager is always crap," I said. "But it gets better." He didn't respond. What was wrong with him?

"You OK, Oliver?" I asked.

"Oh, for fuck's sake," he snapped. "You don't exist; you're an imaginary friend or whatever. Leave me alone."

It was as if he'd punched me in the guts, if I had guts. I

staggered back to the living room. What was the point of my existence, if Oliver didn't believe in me? He was my whole world. I was about to follow him when I noticed that Marjorie's jaw was set hard in an expression that I'd never seen. This should be interesting. When she spoke, her voice had a steel thread running right through it.

"Now he's out of the room, I'm going to tell you straight. I'm glad Rob's out of your life, and so should you be. Oliver told me that Rob whacked him, and when he told you, you accused him of lying."

I knew about the hitting; I'd seen it for myself. It was one of all sorts of reasons I'd come to the conclusion I wasn't here to watch over Oliver. What's the point of a guardian angel that can't stop bad things happening? But that Sarah had accused him of lying ... I leapt over to her and smacked her repeatedly across the head, as if the action would hammer it into her thick skull that she had a son she should be putting first.

"You evil bitch," I shouted. "You don't deserve a son like him."

Sarah shivered and looked around. "Sometimes I swear this bloody house is haunted," she muttered. "I keep telling you to move into a flat. Maybe one of those sheltered accommodation places."

"Stop changing the subject. It's about time you started remembering you're a mother and put that lad first." Marjorie opened her mouth to continue and then closed it. Sarah's hard face had fallen in on itself, making her look young, vulnerable even.

"Mum, there's something else," she said in a low, wobbly voice "I found a lump and I went to the doctor ..."

I listened on with increasing horror. Even Sarah didn't deserve that. And then came guilt. The number of times I'd wished for bad things for happen to Sarah, and now it was the worst thing that could happen to any woman.

I knew from first-hand experience how it would be for Oliver from now on. Over the following two years time slowed down for me again, as Sarah and Oliver moved in with Marjorie, and I watched the woman I'd loathed being slowly eaten away. Those breasts that I'd envied disappeared, as did the hair. There were minor victories – a scan showed not much tumour growth. Then came major setbacks – I'll never forget Sarah's howls when she found out it had spread to her bones and liver. I didn't let Oliver see me during this time – the poor kid was screwed up enough and I didn't want to make it worse. But I could read his mind – that mix of his pain as he watched his mother suffering, mixed with resentment as Sarah demanded everyone's attention. All he could do was stand by and watch as the family tragedy unfolded, at a time when he needed someone to pay him attention. Just like me at that age. It was around that time that Oliver's stammer had started.

Needless to say, I wasn't around at Sarah's deathbed. That would have been too weird, to have a conversation with her ghost, I mean. But I never saw her, afterwards, so I guess she had an instant transition. Straight to hell, perhaps. Sorry, I tried to be charitable about her, but old habits die hard. Illness didn't improve her personality.

I'd gone with Marjorie to Sarah's funeral, watching Oliver from a distance, now looking like a man rather than a boy, but awkward and gangly in his black suit. That had been the most peculiar day. After that first awful night in Highgate cemetery, I'd never been back to look for fellow ghosts. Now, in the East Finchley cemetery, I looked over my shoulder, constantly expecting to see someone. Apart from my own, it was the first time I'd been to the funeral of someone young and I found myself strangely moved, considering how much I'd hated Sarah. Rather than the hymns my Dad had chosen for me, Sarah had pop songs. I recognised one as the song from *Titanic* – I'd watched the DVD with Marjorie. For the first time in ages, I thought about Kirsty. I bet her mum would have chosen pop songs too – her folks were way younger and cooler than mine. Why hadn't I had the chance to go to her funeral? I didn't even know where she was buried. It was probably here – she'd lived just up the road.

After the service was over, I wandered along the gravestones, looking for Kirsty's grave, and then stopped. Oh my God, what was that little kid doing there? He was curled up, asleep in front one of the gravestones. Was he dead or alive? I reached out to touch him, and felt warm, solid flesh. I shook his shoulder, but he didn't move. Then I noticed his clothes – a shirt with a waistcoat and short flannel trousers, like something out of a museum. I crouched down to get a better look to at the gravestone and read the inscription:

Kevin Patterson

1933-1939

Beloved brother and son

Only six when he died? So was this Kevin Patterson, sleeping here for over eighty years? I wandered up and down the lines, and found another, a tiny baby in a shawl. His headstone said. "John Simpson. Born asleep, 1990." The sight and the words were so sad, I couldn't resist lifting him into my arms and giving him a cuddle. Poor baby, all alone all these years. He didn't stir. But he didn't give me the weird maternal pull that Oliver had.

I searched the entire cemetery, and found ten bodies in total. Men, women, all dead before the age of forty, all curled up, asleep in front of their own graves. Then, just as I was giving up hope of finding Kirsty's grave I found it.

"Kirsty!"

There she was, curled up behind the headstone, her head cradled in her long blonde hair. Exactly the way I remembered her. Well, you can imagine how I felt – like I was about to burst. My best friend, lying in front of me. I reached out to touch her. My hands had just made contact with her hair when I stopped. She looked so peaceful, you see. Maybe she was doing what I did – skipping through time. Is this what happened to me – did I go to my own grave to sleep? Maybe it would be dangerous to wake her. Thank God she didn't feel the cold – all she was wearing was leggings and the Johnny Depp T-shirt she used to wear in bed. Still, the thought gave me some comfort. If Kirsty was still around, there was a chance of meeting up with her again.

But where, and how?

And then I felt the dizziness and I skipped a few years of my own.

That just about brings us up to date.

So I hadn't seen Oliver since that day. Would he still be able to see me?

So, three years had passed since I last remember occupying the earth. Had I been lying in a churchyard in Suffolk all this time? What had changed while I'd been away? I needed to investigate. First I checked out the residents of the bedsits. I always enjoyed seeing who was living in my old home – now an Eastern European family with a screaming baby – thank God I had no sense of smell as there were nappy bags everywhere. Then I had a walk down Muswell Hill Broadway. At first glance, little had changed, except that there were more of those boxy vehicles that were half car, half minibus on the road. Why did no-one drive small cars any more? And why were nearly all vehicles silver? Some shops and restaurants had changed hands, others kept their familiar frontages. I looked at newspapers in the stands; 'Gay marriage legalised'. Wow, we were living in a more tolerant age than I remembered. I wondered whether people who looked different from the norm were socially acceptable yet.

Next stop: East Finchley cemetery. I'd memorised the exact location of the children's graves. Kevin had disappeared. Perhaps he'd been waiting for someone? But baby John was still there. And so was Kirsty, and in exactly the same position as she'd been last time. Interesting – did she never wake? I stroked her hair. It felt silky soft as it slid though my fingers.

"Hiya, it's Cyclops," I whispered.

And then it happened again. Dizzy, dizzy, spinning now …

And there I was, back in Marjorie's living room. Sitting on the sofa, head bent over a pile of papers, was a guy, the red hair instantly recognisable.

And I had the feeling that a new adventure was about to begin.

CHAPTER 6

31st March 2014

"Oliver!"

Oliver dropped his papers. "Rowena?" He stood up, allowing me to fully take in his adult appearance.

Wow.

I gawped. Oliver as hunk was not something I'd prepared myself for. He was tall, over six feet, but still kind of awkward in the stoop-shouldered way he held himself, as if he didn't know what to do with his height. His hairstyle – if I could call it that – was a complete mess, the colour now a rich copper. Like me, he wore black – a loose plain sweatshirt and worn black jeans. Perhaps the 'just got out of bed' look was in, but he gave the overall impression of someone who didn't care about appearance. But the scruffy look suited him. His skin was clear except for a light dusting of freckles across his nose that made his eyes appear even bluer. His lips curled into that lopsided smile that still melted me. And he had cheekbones so sharp they could slice tomatoes. In short, he was drop-dead gorgeous. Oh my God. That was the last thing I expected.

"Your voice is so deep," I said.

"I should think so; I'm nineteen." He smiled.

I smiled back, pleased to notice he'd outgrown his stammer. But why wouldn't he look me in the eye?

He rubbed his eyes, then looked to the ceiling. "This is a wind up! You're not real; you're an illusion, brought on by stress." He dropped his head, shook it, but still wouldn't look at me. "Thought I was over all that."

"No, I'm real, that is, if a dead person can be real."

He sat down with a thud and dropped his head in his hands. "That's all I need."

I crouched beside him. "Oliver, it is me. I promise."

He didn't lift his head for some time but eventually he stared at me, but it wasn't a look that said he was happy with what he saw.

"You're shittin' me? You're a – what – a ghost?"

"Yep, got it in one. Don't look so surprised. You never used to question it."

"I was a kid back then. Come on, this is bullshit. Can you prove you're not something I'm imagining?"

I suppose it was a bit much to expect him to be as pleased to see me as I was to see him, but I'd been hoping for more enthusiasm than this.

"I could put my hand through the wall." I demonstrated.

"Nah, I'd expect ghosts to do that."

Then I remembered something else. "All right, Mr Cynic. Come over here." I stood in front of the mirror and he followed me. The only reflection was his. "That enough for you?"

"Yeah, that's pretty cool," he said. "There's no need to sound so pissed off. You can hardly blame me for freaking out. If you're a ghost, why do you do that thing with your hair?"

"What thing?"

"That twisting thing."

I dropped the strand. "I dunno. Nerves? Aren't ghosts allowed to have habits?"

"Don't ask me. You make the rules. Tell me something else. Something I couldn't find out for myself."

"How about this: on the day you were born, I died about there" – I pointed to the base of the staircase – "and whenever I try to go somewhere else, I eventually get dizzy and black out. Next thing I know, I'm right back here, but time's moved on. And sometimes I spy on people. The couple that live in my old bedsit are Eastern European, judging by their accent. She stays at home with a baby that screams a lot and has nappy rash. When she's got him to sleep during the day she sits by her dressing table and puts on all her make-up. It covers up the dark circles under her eyes and transforms her; she looks beautiful. Then she takes it all off and doesn't smile for the rest of the day. The guy in the upstairs flat –"

"OK, I believe you." His eyes went crinkly when he smiled. "Actually, tell me about the guy upstairs."

"He sprays something onto his hair to make it look thicker. And he has his own computer and he looks at pictures of girls – no, not like that, girls with clothes on. It looks like it's a sort of lonely hearts club. He then types messages to them and tells them he's an investment banker, but I think he's lying. There's a badge on his dressing table that says, 'Pete. How can I help you?'."

"Online dating," he said.

"Huh? Oh, never mind. And I've been here for … I just realised today, nineteen years. So we're the same age … at least I assume I stayed nineteen. What do I look like?"

"You look exactly like you do in this photo but with better hair." Funny, that photo had been so flattering. Did both halves of my face look that good? "You've never changed. Sorry, it's a lot to get my head round." His gaze had returned to the carpet.

"I'm so sorry about Marjorie. I was with her when she died. She was asleep; it was peaceful."

"Thanks, that's good to know."

We fell silent for a few moments; I could tell he was choked up.

"I'm still having a hard time with this," he said, when he'd recovered himself. "You kept coming back here, like, for nineteen years? You got some sort of unfinished business or something?"

"I haven't a clue." I shrugged. "I thought I was some sort of guardian angel for your nan, but she passed on and left me behind."

"Nineteen years, a ghost." He scratched his head. "Isn't it kinda lonely?"

"No more than most people's lives. And I haven't been conscious for nineteen years, more like a year or so. After I black out and wake up here, time's moved on. The last time I saw you was at your mum's funeral when you were sixteen."

"Ah, so that's why I didn't always see you."

"Sometimes I was here, but I hid. I saw the effect I was having on you and I didn't want anyone marking you out as different. And then that time when you dismissed me as an imaginary friend, I thought I was messing with your head too much. You had enough to cope with."

"I used to love seeing you. I remember you telling me it made me special." He ran his hand through his hair. "Huh, I still can't believe I'm having this conversation. So … what's it like? Being a ghost, I mean? Got any other cool tricks?"

"Not really. People feel something when I touch them. It sort of makes them shiver. I can scare people off. And I seem to have a sense of when and where I'm needed. I turned up whenever Marjorie was in danger." I told him about the muggers. "And once I got onto a tube train with her. She was always kind of nervous of taking the tube. It was busy and no-one offered her a seat. So I crouched opposite a youngish guy in a suit and yelled at him, "What's wrong with you? You'd let an old lady stand?" He stood up and gave up his seat. But when I spoke to him as I'm speaking now, he didn't hear me. I tried shouting again, but I guess I needed to be pissed off."

Oliver laughed. "So you always looked out for Nan?"

"Yeah, I'm going to miss her."

"Me too," he said, our eyes meeting for the first time. "She was the only person who really got me, apart from you."

His gaze was disconcerting.

"When you hit people, do you feel anything?" he asked.

"I sometimes feel a bit queasy if someone walks through me. But otherwise, no. I don't feel heat or cold. I never feel a thing," except you, I stopped myself from saying. How could I tell him that he was the only solid object I could touch? He looked like his head was about to explode already.

But his thought process was clearly working overtime. "When I was a kid, I remember you telling me that I was the only person who could see or hear you. That can't be right?"

I twisted my hair again. He'd know if I was lying. "Seems that way. I've wandered all over London, shouting at people, but nothing." I told him about that night in Highgate and about seeing the kids in Finchley.

"This is seriously screwed up," he muttered. "Why me?"

"I've no idea. You were born on the day I died." I paused. I'd thought about this a million times before, so why I thought the answer would come this time, I don't know. "But you were born first, so I don't see how that connects us."

"Thank God for that. I thought you were about to say that part of you had reincarnated into me or something."

"I wondered if it because it was because you were a kid, and you'd grow out of it, but I walked past a school once, and none of the kids saw me." His expression changed and I was reminded of that frightened boy again. Perhaps I'd better change the subject. "Sorry. I know it's a lot to take in. You've come to clear this place out, I guess?"

"Yeah. Hard to know where to start. Perhaps the things I'm going to keep, first."

He took the photo of me down from the wall. A thrill passed through me – he wanted to keep my photo?

"I once asked Nan why you had your hair like this. That's before I'd seen the Human League on YouTube. Tragic decade, the eighties."

"What's YouTube?"

"Huh, you really have been gone for nineteen years, haven't you? Anyway, Nan said you were scarred. But you're not."

"Oh, I was. Horribly. And I only had one eye."

"Bloody hell. What happened?"

"A chip pan fire. My mum died of a brain tumour. Just before it was diagnosed, she used to get headaches and started behaving oddly. I was thirteen. I found her in the kitchen, just standing there, watching the fire. Luckily, I knew what to do – I'd seen it on telly. I got a tea towel, soaked it in water and wrung it out. I was just about to put it over the pan when Mum kinda came back to life, picked up a pan of water, and flung it on the fire. Worst thing you can do. It flared up in my face. I was burnt from here" – I pointed to the spot above my right eyebrow – "to here." I placed my hand an inch below my cheekbone. "My face was a hell of a mess afterwards. My eye socket was so damaged that they couldn't put in an artificial eye, and I had no eyebrow. My mouth turned up like this" – I deliberately jerked my lips at one side – "because the skin tightened when it healed."

"I never realised it was that bad. Nan never described it in detail. Hard to imagine, looking at you now. Your face is so … perfect."

I wondered whether my face had gone red; I didn't feel the heat that normally went with blushing, but inside I was burning. I picked up the picture of Marjorie and Oliver at the zoo. "This is my favourite," I said. "Remember that weekend?"

"Course I do!" He grinned. "I nearly wet myself laughing when you got into the lion pit and made it roar."

"The zookeepers must have wondered what was going on – I managed to upset every animal there. I guess animals see me; dogs often bark when I pass by. Remember how I kept pulling faces behind the waxworks at Madame Tussaud's and made you laugh?"

"Yeah."

My voice dropped. "You were going through a rotten time at school back then, weren't you? I guess it got better? I skipped a few years."

He lifted a hand to his hair. "Yeah, the teasing stopped when I got in the football team. Then I started growing. They don't pick on you so much if you're bigger than them."

"I used to worry about you," I said. "I'm so glad I got to see you again. It'll be strange to have someone else living here."

"Well … I was thinking of moving in. It's mine now, and it's nicer than my bedsit. Handy for college."

And that's when I put two and two together and made a million and nine. Maybe that's why I kept coming back to this house. I knew that one day it'd be Oliver's. And that by then, he'd be the right age for me. I'd been waiting for him.

"You OK?" he asked.

"Er … yeah. You're at college? Fantastic. I always wanted to go. What do you do?"

"I'm at Imperial College, studying IT," he said. I frowned – the letters meant nothing to me. "That's computers."

Computers? Oliver had turned out to be a genius. And, if my snooping around the neighbours was typical, everyone seemed to have them these days, so it must be a good area to work in.

"So you worked in a bookshop?" he asked.

"Yeah, I loved books; I'd planned to study English Literature at university. But my mum died on the day of my first GCSE so I never took any of them. When I moved here, I went to night school and resat them. I'd been studying for A levels when I died."

"So unfair. Life dealt you a shitty hand of cards." His expression was the saddest thing I'd ever seen. I had to resist the urge to take his hand. And then a bolt of sanity hit me. Of course I couldn't be here to have a relationship with Oliver. He inhabited the land of the living. He might even – the thought made me heave – have a girlfriend.

"Well, if you're going to move in, I'd better warn you. I think I still live here. It wasn't a problem for your nan – she never saw me – but it might be for you. I'm not here all the time; I come and go. But I wouldn't get in your way. I mean … if you brought a girl back, I could go out for a walk. I'm unpredictable too. You never know, you might be thirty by the time you see me again. Just thought you ought to know. You might want to live somewhere less … haunted."

"I don't suppose I'll be bringing a girl back any time soon." He stared at the carpet then raised his eyes to hold my gaze. "And I'd kinda like having you around."

My hopes soared sky high. Could I really stay with Oliver? Get to know him properly?

"Don't leave it so long next time though, will you?" he asked.

Maybe I was here for a reason!

CHAPTER 7

31st March 2014

After Oliver left the flat, I paced up and down, thoughts cartwheeling in my head. Usually, after Marjorie had left the house for the evening or gone to bed, I'd disappear, as if I'd fallen asleep, and reappear in the living room, not knowing what day, month, or even year it was. Now, for the first time since my early days, I was restless. What was I here for? My fate must be tied up with Oliver. But how and why?

I needed answers, and there was only one place where I might get them: a cemetery. I'd never seen any ghosts in Finchley other than the sleeping kids. Maybe Highgate would be a better bet – it was way bigger. You'd think I'd have been back again in all this time, wouldn't you? But my first experience had freaked me out so much, I just couldn't face it. Tonight, I was feeling brave. Besides, what was the worst that could happen? I'd end up here again. I raced over there before I had time to lose my nerve. It was twilight, the lime green canopy of the new spring leaves still bright, making the atmosphere a lot less intimidating than last time. I tiptoed through the field of graves, and peered around each stone but saw nothing.

"Aren't there any friendly ghosts out there?" I kept my voice low.

Then I saw a man sprawled across a grave in what I'm pretty sure was a drunken stupor. You have to remember I didn't know – I'd never even been drunk. Was he a ghost or a homeless? I moved closer and wrinkled my nose at his matted hair and stain-encrusted overcoat; I could smell the alcohol on him. Hang on – I hadn't smelt anything for years! I knelt by his side and placed my hand on his shoulder. Yes, his body felt solid. But should I go any further? He didn't look any more promising than the biker.

"Hello," I said. "Can you hear me?"

The man shuddered, rolled over, scratched his head and sat upright. He had what you might call a grizzled face – all white stubble and leathery skin. His hair was wiry and a salt-and-pepper colour. His eyebrows were the colour and texture of Brillo pads. I wouldn't like to guess his age – I could be decades out.

"Bloody hell, don't you know better than to wake the dead?" I couldn't help laughing. It was his accent, the drawling Northern sort that came right out of Emmerdale or Coronation Street – I could never tell the difference. And also the fact that he still sounded slightly drunk.

"Sorry," I whispered. "I've never met anyone ... like us before."

The man stood up, swayed, and leaned on the gravestone for support. "Aw shit, you're just a bairn. Me name's Frank." He held out his hand. I took it and kept hold, shocked by the solidity of his grip.

"OK, you can let go now," he said, but his lips had twitched upwards.

"I just can't believe it – so long since I felt someone's hand. I'm Rowena. Why can I touch you?"

"Christ, you're a new 'un, aren't you? Course I'm not solid flesh. Neither of us are, but because we're the same form, or whatever you wanna call it, we feel what we expect to feel."

"So why can't we feel other people?"

"Because we're trapped in the wrong world." His voice was matter-of-fact, as if all this should be obvious.

"Why didn't I know this? I'm not new at all. I was pushed down the steps and broke my neck in 1995."

"I fell under a train at Archway, 1985. Mind you, I were pissed at the time." Frank grinned.

I shuddered. "Ugh, nasty way to go."

"You're seriously telling me that you've been around all these years, and you haven't met any others like us? Where the hell have you been?"

"In Muswell Hill." I grinned. "I wasn't always around. I've skipped a lot of time, including the last three years."

"A sleeper, eh?" he asked, scratching the stubble on his

chin. "That often happens with young 'uns. Toddlers sometimes sleep here fifty years or more until their parents are about to pass."

"That figures. I had a friend who died a year after me. She's asleep in Finchley. I saw a couple of small kids sleeping there. That's the only other cemetery I've been to. I came here, soon after I died, but this horrible ghost yelled at me. Scared the hell out of me. He was a biker with half his face smashed in, must've been about my age. Then a woman had a go at me too."

"The biker sounds like Tommy Judd. Always was a lairy little shit. He was smacked off his tits when he came off his bike. Christ, I'd forgotten all about him. He passed on more than fifteen years ago. I guess you came in here shouting?"

I nodded.

"First lesson for you - don't raise your voice in a cemetery; there's others trying to sleep. It's a resting place, not a social club. The Heath's a good place to go at night if you want to meet people like us. What are you here for?"

"Well, a cemetery seemed the logical place –"

"Not here. I mean here as in on earth. Why haven't you passed over?"

"That's what I'm trying to work out."

"Ah well, if it's a good natter you're after, how about you and me go for a walk?"

It looked like the best offer I was likely to get. Frank rose to his feet, stirring up a massive waft of distillery, and together we strolled to Hampstead Heath. Along the way, I told him how, until last week, I'd assumed Marjorie was my reason for staying.

"No-one else you're waiting for?" He frowned. "Parents? Boyfriend?"

"No, my parents are already dead and I didn't have a boyfriend. Why are you here?"

"Waiting for me missus. Jean. She didn't cope, y'see. Needed me to stay. That's how it is with most people who don't pass over. But there must have been someone crying for you."

"No, Mum died three years before me. Dad – well, we weren't close. Marjorie and my best friend Kirsty – the one who died – were probably the only ones who cried at my funeral."

"Hmm, has to be more than that, or you'd have passed over when one of them did. They say people can stick around for other reasons. One thing … not summat I've come across … Were there something you didn't do in life, summat really important, that you always wanted to do?"

I twisted my hair so tightly I thought I'd pull it out. Yes there was, but how could I say it out loud?

"Spit it out, lass. No sense in being embarrassed after you're dead now, is there?"

"I'd never … been kissed," I murmured.

"Aww, you're kidding?" He smoothed down his coat and puffed out his chest. "How old were you? Seventeen? Eighteen?"

"Nineteen." How much hotter could my face get?

"Well, love, I'd oblige meself but I'm a one woman man. Faithful to Jean, even in death. Not many women that can say that about their husbands now, is there?"

"That's lovely," I said. Eeuww, just as well. Frank was hardly the stuff of fantasy.

"Can't believe a pretty little thing like you lived on this earth for nineteen years without finding yourself a fella," Frank's eyes were twinkling. "Grew up in a convent, did you?"

"No. But I wasn't quite so pretty." I told him about the accident.

"Aw, love, life's bloody cruel sometimes."

"That's another thing I don't get. Why aren't I scarred now?" I asked. "That motorcyclist guy – he was hideous."

"Never quite understood that meself. Some people look better in death, some worse, others about the same. I reckon you were a nice lass, good to others, am I right?"

"I guess so …"

"There you go, then. Inner beauty or whatever they call it. As you can see, I wasn't exactly a saint in life."

"I guess not." I grinned "Oh, it's so fantastic to have someone to talk to. I've got so much to ask. If you go far from home, do you sort of spin back?"

"Course I do. We all do. Everyone has a place that pulls them."

"Why can I sit on a sofa and it feels solid underneath me, but if I try and touch it with my hands, they sink in?"

"Hands are different. Some of us can even pick things up. I can, look." He lifted a daffodil.

"Why can you do that but I can't?"

"Dunno. Seems to me, dead people all have different levels of ability, just like living people. I was a carpenter, used to work with me hands. Maybe that's why?"

"I guess that makes sense."

My head span. All this time, with nothing explained to me, and now Frank was answering all my questions as if this stuff was common knowledge.

"There's one other thing …"

"Go on." He grinned, showing a row of chipped teeth.

"It's Marjorie's grandson, Oliver … He was born on the day I died. Ever since he was a baby, he could see, hear, and even touch me. And I could touch him. Until I met you, he was the only solid object I could touch. Now he's the same age as me. And he's inherited Marjorie's house. He's going to move in."

What had I said? Frank's eyebrows had raised almost to his hairline.

"He can touch you? I've heard a lot of peculiar stories over the years, but never that before. And he feels solid, like I do?"

I nodded.

"Hmm, that's a rum 'un. Jean only sees and hears me every now and again. The only time I tried putting my arm around her, me hands went straight through her."

"That's why I was looking for someone tonight, for some answers. I think maybe my fate's tangled up with Oliver's. I spoke to him earlier and warned him that I might be living there. I though he'd freak at the idea of a haunted house, but it turns out he wants me there."

"Hmm …" The groove between his eyes deepened. "Tell you what, I know someone who might be able to help. Hippy dippy woman, one of those – what do they call 'em these days – New Age types. Come over here at night; I'm usually around. You can yell all you like there."

We chatted some more, and then Frank said he needed to

get back. Apparently all ghosts needed to sleep, some more than others.

"If you're ever desperate to talk to someone, I sleep here a lot of the time." He waved his hand over the grave. A fresh bunch of daffodils had recently been placed in a metal container. I read the inscription on his headstone:

Frank MacLean

Died 1985, aged 57 years

Beloved husband and father

"You had children, too?" I asked.

"Yeah, two lads. I've got grandkids now as well, three of 'em. Didn't live to meet 'em, but I've seen 'em when they've been visiting Jean."

Lucky Frank. He'd left a mark on the world. That was the worst thing about dying so young. I'd had an impact on people's lives – all those people at my funeral had been proof of that – but I hadn't left anything permanent. No children, no great discoveries or works of art or anything that I'd be remembered for. I guess my nieces and nephews might tell their children in future that they had a tragic scarred aunt who died a heroine, but did I want tragedy to be my legacy?

"And don't waste time feeling sorry for yourself," Frank said. "Them that hang around do so for a reason, but it might take a whole lifetime to find out what it is. Now, off with you; we don't want to be waking the dead. You know where to find me."

I said goodbye with a pang of disappointment, but also a massive thrill. What a day! In all this time as a ghost I'd had next to no conversations. Today I'd had two.

CHAPTER 8

8th April, 2014

I'd walked back after that, and had almost reached home before the head spins got to me. I woke on a leather chair – the sofa had disappeared – to find Oliver stripping off the anaglypta that had been a constant feature of this room for the last nineteen years. All of Marjorie's furniture and clutter had gone. The room looked twice the size.

"Wow, it's going to be different in here," I said.

He swung around.

"Rowena! Hi, I wondered where you were."

"I'm a rubbish guest, I'm afraid." It hit me all of a sudden that now I was a guest. This place that I'd come to think of at home was getting a complete new look. I shrugged apologetically. "No warnings; I just appear randomly."

"So you're a ghost with no manners, as well crap clothes. Do you ever take those slippers off?"

"If I'd have realised I'd be spending eternity in the same outfit, I'd have put on my prom dress that night."

"Hope you were wearing your best underwear." He winked. Funny, I'd expected Oliver to be kind of shy and awkward, but he wasn't at all.

"That's for me to know and you to find out." I winked back. What was I doing? I'd never spoken like that in my life.

"A flirty ghost too, eh? This could be interesting." He sat down next to me on the sofa, his expression becoming serious. "I was worried you might have … what d'you call it … passed on."

"Why, how long is it since I last saw you? Have you moved in?"

"A week. No, I want to get the place into shape before I

move in. Bring it into the twenty-first century. But I'm staying here tonight. I was hoping you'd show up. It's Nan's funeral tomorrow. Will you – God, this sounds silly – will you be able to make it?"

"My diary's free." I smiled. "Seriously though, I guess that's why I turned up. I'm always around for the important things, whether I know they're about to happen or not. When your nan started with those chest pains, four or five years ago, I used to go with her to the doctor's appointments. She hated going to the doctor's. I was probably kidding myself, but I think I helped her by being there, calmed her down a bit.

"You did. At Mum's funeral, I thought I saw you, at the back of the church."

I nodded. "It didn't seem right to speak to you; you had enough to deal with."

"Afterwards, I mentioned it to Nan. Mum hated me mentioning your name, but Nan understood. She said she'd often felt there was someone else in the house. Sometimes she'd get herself worked up about something then she'd feel calm for no reason."

"I didn't tell you last time, but she spoke to me, just before she passed over." I explained. "And she looked so young, you wouldn't believe it." I told him the story of our last encounter.

"I'm glad she got to speak to you. Wasn't long though, was it? Looking after her all those years, you deserved more."

"Don't make me out to be some sort of saint. I didn't have much choice."

"But you did when you were alive. She told me how much you did for her."

"Ah, well, she never had a problem with my face. You see, I had trouble making friends, looking the way I did. All my friends came from the Sunlight centre – that was a day centre for teenagers with all sorts of disabilities. You know the sort of thing – misfits of the world unite. It was a brilliant place though; I noticed around ten years ago that it's shut down. Marjorie found it for me in the first place – she was like a mother to me. And it's funny, we didn't have much in common except for watching old black-and-white films, but I liked being with her."

"Yeah, she was easy company; she did all the talking." We both smiled. "But why did you become her guardian angel? My granddad died the year before you, didn't he? Wouldn't he have been the logical choice?"

"She asked me the same question. I knew your granddad too, he was a lovely man. But he died of natural causes, a heart attack. Maybe that's it. He probably passed quickly, like your nan did."

"Makes sense. Must be scary for you though, not knowing when it's all going to end."

"It is, sometimes." Especially since I had more of a reason to stay around. Oliver was relaxed, his smile freer, and I couldn't drag my gaze from those deep blue eyes. "Oh, guess what. I went back to the cemetery and found a ghost to talk to."

"Cool! Did you ask him why I'm the only one that can see you?"

"Yeah ... he wasn't much help. But he did say that different ghosts had different abilities. He can move objects. Wish I could. How much fun would that be?"

"Yeah ... that'd be awesome, freaking people out. So what's the first thing you'd do, if you could move objects?"

It was a simple conversation, the sort that you'd take for granted. But for me, it was a miracle. It was so long since I'd chatted that my words tumbled out. Thank God Oliver wasn't as awkward as he used to be. Why didn't he have women queuing round the block? He was funny and charming but in a thoughtful, self-deprecating way. But I couldn't help thinking of the irony of the situation. If I'd met Oliver in life, he was exactly the sort of guy I'd have fallen for, and if he'd met me in real life, he wouldn't have been able to see past my scarred face. Or would he? He seemed like he was still sensitive – maybe he'd have been above appearances.

He returned to stripping the wallpaper but we didn't stop talking, not for a minute. I'd missed some parts of his life and wanted to fill in every missing piece of the jigsaw.

"You never seemed to get on with your Mum," I said. "But to lose her that way must have been rough on you."

"It was, but I guess you went through the same. Did your

Mum have chemo?"

"Yeah, I remember seeing strands of her hair in the sink after she washed it. Horrible. At least the wigs have improved over the years. Your mum's wasn't bad."

"She hated it. It was shitty to watch her like that." He shrugged. "In the last few months she just sort of gave up. And then afterwards, I felt guilty that I didn't feel more – know what I mean? I don't think she'd ever wanted kids; I think I'd been an accident in the first place. And then … I always seemed to be in the way, stopped her from living her life the way she wanted to."

"I know exactly what you mean. I wasn't planned either. Mum was forty-six, and my brothers and sisters were more than ten years older than me. My folks weren't happy about me turning up. I buggered up Dad's retirement plan."

I shivered with the memory. I'd heard the argument from the bedroom. I'd been twelve and Dad had just been offered the chance to retire.

"You can forget that," Mum had said. "You'll be working until you're sixty-five. You blew any chances of affording early retirement twelve years ago when you couldn't keep it zipped up."

"Don't blame me," Dad retorted. "Bloody Dr Day's fault. So much for you being in the change."

"They shouldn't have done that to you. They shouldn't have blamed you," Oliver said.

"Huh? Did you just read my mind?"

"I worked it out. Funny, I feel I know you so well already. Both of us not wanted. I used to wish I could come and live here with you and Nan."

"You got half your wish."

And we carried on that way, realising that we already knew each other more intimately than seemed possible, since we'd never had a long conversation before. You know the way that the life stories we tell when getting to know someone are never unbiased and rarely accurate? Well, with Oliver, it wasn't like that. I felt no need to hide anything and, judging by the painful honesty of his words, the same was true for him. When he finished painting the walls, he ordered a pizza, which looked way better than anything Marjorie ever ate. Never had I had a stronger urge to eat.

"It looks fantastic," I said. "At least I can't smell it. That would be torture."

"Funny, I'd almost forgotten. You seem so real to me," he murmured. "I just can't believe you're not." Our gazes locked for a few moments longer than was comfortable. Right now, I wished more than anything that I could be alive, sharing his pizza ... and more. For the first time, we fell into an uncomfortable silence. When he finished eating, I pointed at an unfamiliar object on the coffee table.

"What's that?"

"It's a tablet, a sort of computer. I'll show you."

He handed it to me, then laughed when it passed straight through my hands,

"OK, Moaning Myrtle, I'll hold it. Shuffle up, so you can see."

I sat so close that our thighs were almost touching, and, with a strange shiver, realised I was aware of his scent. How could I smell him, and yet not the pizza? Frank said that spirits felt what they expected to feel. All my senses had been intact as far as Frank was concerned, right down to the whisky breath. It was almost as if Oliver, too, was a ghost. Change the subject. Focus on the tiny computer that seemed to have no keyboard.

"It looks cool, but what do you do with it?" she asked.

"Everything. I can get my e-mails, look at Facebook, watch videos, play games, browse online," Oliver said.

"OK, slow down. Not one word of that made sense. It's like you're talking a different language."

"Hell, yeah – did you even have in computers back in – when did you – hang on, of course, 1995. Year I was born. You're wearing well for an old woman. But surely you had the internet back then?"

"Thanks – I think. Computers were around, but I didn't have one. We had one at the bookshop for cataloguing. There was talk of setting up a website and we had e-mail, but I didn't use it. And the computers were nothing like this."

"Welcome to the twenty-first century. Anything you ever

need to know, instantly. Here's the latest news." He tapped on one of the little squares on the screen and instantly, a picture of a beautiful mixed race girl appeared. *JASMINE: SEARCH INTENSIFIES*, the heading read.

"Wow, that's incredible," I said. "What's happened to the girl?"

"She's been missing for over a month. Only eighteen."

"That's sad ... So what else does this gadget do? Things I'd understand."

"Let's see," Oliver scratched his chin. "You can communicate with other people, discuss books, that sort of thing. You can study anything you like."

I grinned. "I think you might have the wrong idea about me. Just because I worked in a bookshop doesn't make me an intellectual. I read plenty, but a lot of it was trashy, escapist fiction."

"I'm not exactly an intellectual either. You like music?"

"Love it."

At another tap of the screen, music started, and it was something I recognised.

"Hey, I've heard this before. The Smiths isn't it? How come you like this? It's before my time, even."

"You can access anything these days," he said. "And I love these guys. I like the way their music takes you outside the ordinary. As if Morrissey looked inside your head and said, hey, it's OK to be lonely." He looked down.

I gave him an encouraging smile, hoping he'd continue. He'd encapsulated in a few words the reason certain music moved me so profoundly. But no, he'd closed down, as if he'd unintentionally revealed too much of himself and now he was closing the curtains. But what he'd said didn't quite add up. How could Oliver be lonely? He seemed so self-assured. Maybe he was saying it to make me feel better. But as I looked at him, I could see the emptiness inside him. Did he have no friends? It seemed an insensitive question to ask. We listened to a few more Smiths songs, the lyrics resonating with each of us in a way neither needed to voice to the other.

"Your turn now," he said. Anything you like. Who was your first crush?"

"George Michael."

"That really is sad." He tapped the screen. "Here he is. *Careless Whisper*. What's going on with his hair?"

"Don't say anything bad about George; I was deeply in love with him. Who was your first crush?"

"Cheryl Cole."

"Who's she?"

He showed me.

"Nah, I'm much better. What does Johnny Depp look like these days?" I instinctively reached for the screen, and accidentally brushed against his hand. We both flinched.

"Whoa, what happened there? Shouldn't your hand go straight through mine?" he said.

"I didn't want to freak you out, but this has happened before. When you were a baby, you grasped my finger, and I felt it. When you were eight and stayed with your Nan that weekend, upset about the bullies, I crept into your room and talked to you while you were sleeping. I stroked your hair."

"No way? This is seriously creepy."

"I don't know why it happens. I asked Frank, the ghost in Highgate. I'm able to shake hands with him, smell whisky on him, everything. He said that's normal between ghosts, because we feel what we expect to feel. But he'd never come across a ghost who could touch a human and vice versa."

He lifted his hand towards my face.

"Is it OK if I …?"

I nodded.

His hands traced the contours of my face, slowly and deliberately. The tenderness of his touch gave me a peculiar shiver.

"I don't get it," he said "You feel warm, exactly as if you were alive." He placed a finger under my nostrils. "But I can't feel your breathing."

"Your senses are telling you I should be warm, so I am. Bet you can't feel my pulse either." I turned my wrist towards him. His fingers pressed against me, exploring the blood vessels visible through my pale skin. He pulled away, shaking his head.

"Can I touch your face?" I asked.

"Go ahead."

I stroked the smooth skin of his cheekbones and moved my

fingers down towards his chin, taking in the faint rasp of stubble. And I guess it was fair to say my feelings for him weren't maternal any more. In fact, I'd never felt anything close to the way I was feeling right now, sort of lightheaded and – I know how stupid this sounds – *alive*. Like I wanted to dance round the room, but at the same time I didn't want to move away from him. Ever. And there it was again – the scent of him. Was I imagining it?

"What's up?" he said. "You look like … ha, I was going to say you look like you've seen a ghost."

"I can smell you."

"Oh no." He sniffed his armpits. "What do I smell like?"

"I'm not sure how to describe it. Kind of sweet and warm. I guess it's the smell of fresh sweat." How could I tell him that I was imagining laying my head on his chest, closing my eyes and losing myself in that smell?

He moved his face close to mine, studying every detail of my face, like he was memorising it for an exam. He moved down to my neck and throat and then upwards so that his nose almost touched my hair. I'd never realised how physical a look could be. My head started to swim. Better move away – I didn't want to disappear and find a year had passed.

"Sorry," I said. "I got a strange feeling, like I do when I'm about to disappear, but worse."

"No, don't go. Not now. Here, lie down, rest or whatever you need to do."

He placed a cushion at one end of the sofa and I lay down.

"Better?"

"Yeah." The room slowly returned into full focus.

"B-but, I could smell you too, Rowena. Your neck … I don't know. Something orangey."

I gasped as a long-forgotten memory returned. "That day, when I was killed, I had a shower after I got back from work. The shower gel – I think it was bergamot."

Neither of us spoke, then we both spoke together.

"How is this possible?"

CHAPTER 9

9th April, 2014

I marched around the Heath, one of my favourite places in London. I used to love the views over the city, not that I could see much in the blackness, only a tiny sliver of moon illuminating the way.

"Frank, you here?" I cried.

How could I have been so stupid? I'd never find him – the Heath was vast. I guess I could go to the cemetery and see if he was asleep … no, that wasn't fair. Maybe I'd find someone else, perhaps even the woman Frank mentioned. Somebody had to make sense of this for me.

Oliver was freaking out, even though he didn't admit it. After what happened yesterday, he'd shifted across to the end of the sofa and we'd spent evening in what felt like safer territory, watching TV. At eleven, he'd said.

"Well, I'm gonna turn in now. So … I guess you stay here?"

"Yeah, I just disappear when I'm tired," I said. "Don't worry; I'll be back in the morning."

For the first time, I'd laid on the sofa in the dark for hours, terrified that if I left, I wouldn't re-materialise for Marjorie's funeral. I'd never tried to turn up to order before. At some stage sleep – or my version of it – overtook me and when I reappeared it was nine-thirty in the morning and Oliver was looking in the mirror, straightening his tie. Thank God. I'd crept up behind him and tapped him on the shoulder.

"That's a low trick," he'd said. "Sneaking up on me when I can't see your reflection."

The funeral had left us both feeling wrung out. The church was half-filled – Marjorie had been popular but had outlived most of her family. It was a beautiful service though; one her friends from the senior citizen's club had given a moving speech about the colour she brought into her life. But only a handful of people stayed for the burial – some of them were so frail they could barely stand – and Oliver looked so alone, blinking in an attempt not to cry, that I'd slipped my hand into his. Holding hands felt so *right*, a perfect fit, as if the two of us had literally been made for each other. No, mustn't think like that. I'd already labelled them my 'Mills and Boon' moments – these mushy thoughts I had every time I saw him. He was alive; I wasn't. Afterwards we'd returned home, listened to music, and spent all evening reminiscing about Marjorie. And now I needed to talk about these Mills and Boon moments with someone. Preferably someone who'd tell me that it was okay to fall in love with a living being.

"Frank, where are you?" I shouted, even though I doubted that the old drunk would think much of me gushing like a soppy teenager. But hey, I suppose I still was.

I wandered up towards Kenwood House – there was more light up there. But still I found no-one. Then, just as I was giving up hope, my noise attracted someone else. A girl around my age was staring at me, her face screwed up. She looked vaguely familiar – then I remembered. It was the missing girl from the news headline. She was even better looking in the flesh. But hang on, if she could see me ...

"Hi, are you a ghost?" the girl asked, her words coming out at a million miles a minute. Like me, she was tall, but so slim she hardly had any curves. She'd certainly chosen better clothes to die in than me – a white leather jacket, silver sparkly top, short skirt, black tights and high, high heels. She looked like a model.

"Yeah. You're the one who's been on the TV, aren't you? So you died ... that's so sad."

"Yeah, I'm Jasmine," said the girl. "S'not fair – I'm only seventeen. And I'm shit scared and I dunno what to do. You're, like, the first ghost I've seen. Why doesn't no-one tell you what to do? I know what I wanna do, but I can't. I've been looking somewhere different every night, trying to get help. Can you help me?" Why did she talk so quickly, each sentence rising at the end so it sounded like a question?

"I'll try," I said.

"I need the police to find my body, else my mum and dad and brothers won't rest, yeah? I've been back home, but no-one, like hears or sees me. My Mum's been to the doctor's; she's taking these pills now. She don't sleep at night – I see her crying. But I dunno how to tell her."

"I have someone who hears me. Tell me and maybe he can tell them." I regretted the words as soon as they were out of my mouth. Oliver would seriously freak if he knew what I'd volunteered him for.

"I'll show you; s'not far."

We walked out of the Heath towards Highgate.

"So what happened to you?" I asked.

"My scumbag boyfriend done it – yeah, make sure everyone knows that too. Will Johnson. Fucking loser. I was gonna dump him anyway. You know why he did it?"

I shook my head.

"Some guy was coming on to me in the pub. Will was giving me grief all the way back. Then when we got off the tube, he said I had to prove that I loved him. Said I had to do it with him in the woods. So I did, and he just wouldn't stop, you know? He was well rough. I told him I wanted to stop, but he kept going so I tried to push him off. Then he started pressing down on my neck, and he wouldn't let go." Jasmine's voice rose to a higher pitch than I thought possible, then she started crying, great, heaving sobs that shook her whole body.

I gave her a hug. The novelty of being able to touch anyone was still so new that I didn't want to let her go. God, she was skinny – I could feel her shoulder blades jutting through her jacket.

"He murdered you…"

"He didn't mean it, y'know? Afterwards he kept on crying, but there was nothing I could do. Just watched as he hid my body."

"Such a waste," I said.

"My bezzy mate set up this awesome Facebook tribute site for me," Jasmine said. "I saw my brother looking at it. It's had over a thousand likes already. How old are you?"

"I was nineteen when I died but if I was alive I'd be thirty-eight."

"You're shittin' me? That's immense!"

Jasmine continued talking, but it was a lot to take in. She seemed to belong to a different generation, which I suppose she did. But if I'd added up all the days I'd been hanging around as a ghost, as opposed to sleeping by my grave or whatever I did when time whizzed by without me – it would only add up to a year or two. So that made me twenty-one, tops, in terms of life experience. Next to this girl I felt old, uncool. And yet there'd been no barrier between Oliver and me. Obviously I'd missed plenty in terms of fashion and technology, but he never made me feel out of it, the way this girl did. It wasn't just the way she never stopped talking about Snapchat, Instagram and Facebook – I must ask Oliver what they were – it was the details of her relationship with Will. Technology may have advanced, but feminism had gone backwards, it seemed.

"It sounds like he never treated you with any respect," I said. "You mean he expected to sleep with you on the same date?"

"I ain't never slept with him – you think my folks would let him stay the night? I used to suck him off behind the kebab shop."

"So what was in it for you?"

"He was fuckin' hot. Everyone wanted to be with him."

I shuddered. Perhaps I hadn't missed out on as much as I thought. It wouldn't be like that with Oliver. I was being offered a pure, perfect love, a kind that no boy offered in real life. There I go, Mills and Boon again.

When we reached the centre of Queen's Wood, Jasmine pointed to a mound of earth, leaves and twigs under a large tree.

"That's me under there, see?" Jasmine said.

I paced distances and made a mental map of the location. "Don't worry. Go for a walk on Parliament Hill every night and I'll meet you there as soon as I have some news."

My work for the night must have been done. I felt the light-headedness that meant I was leaving and woke in Oliver's living room, to find him painting the wall.

"Hi, what day is it?" I asked.

"Saturday. I saw you a couple of days ago." He ran his

hand through his hair, leaving a streak of buttermilk emulsion.

"Thank God. I need you to do something for me. I met another ghost on the night of the funeral. It was Jasmine, that missing girl that's all over the news."

He put down the roller and shook his head. "Oh shit, so she's dead. That sucks."

"She needs her family to know, and to bring her killer to justice. Can you tell the police?"

He took a step backwards. "Hang on, think about it. How will they take me seriously? I can't exactly walk into a police station and say a ghost told me, can I? And what if they think I'm something to do with it?"

"Can't you make an anonymous call from a phone box?"

He grinned and shook his head. "Can't remember the last time I saw a phone box." Then he sat down and was silent for a while. "OK, I know what we'll do. We need to go shopping first."

Half an hour later, I found myself in a shop filled with mobile phones.

"A whole shop, just for phones?" I giggled. "And how do you dial the number? They're just small version of that – what d'you call it – tablet."

He rolled his eyes, whispered, "Old git," and strode to the counter. "Yeah, just a pay as you go SIM pack please, I've got a handset."

"What on earth does that mean?"

"You'll see," he muttered. "Let's go to Alexandra Palace. It's a pretty anonymous location."

I followed him and watched him replace a tiny card in the back of his phone, then took out the instructions I'd given him. He dialled 999 and took a deep breath. When he spoke, his voice was a low hiss and he spoke in a Scottish accent. Clever.

"Police, please … I've got some information about Jasmine Fletcher. Her boyfriend killed her, Will Johnson, age 20, address 12 Bluebell Towers, Hornsey. He strangled her and hid the body in Queen's Wood in Highgate. Take the path that runs diagonally from the café into the centre of the wood. You take the right hand path at the first junction, then go about fifty paces along, turn off the path and walk to the right about twenty paces until you see a yew tree. Her body's under that."

He clicked the phone shut, took a deep breath and gave her a triumphant smile.

"Oliver, you're brilliant!" I grabbed his arm.

"Did you ever doubt it?" He extracted the card from the back of the phone, took a pair of scissors from his pocket and cut the card in half. "We need to get home so I can destroy this properly."

"Genius," I whispered.

"That was the scariest thing I've ever done in my life. Gave me a hell of a buzz though. Maybe me and you can team up, bring murderers to justice."

"They could make a TV show about us. Or has that already been done?"

He grinned and reached to take my hand.

"You're going to look strange to passers-by with your hand sticking out like that," I said.

"S'pose so. I know, put your hand in my jacket pocket." We linked hands inside the jacket, and my palm tingled with the thrill of the contact.

"I was going to watch a film this evening. Fancy joining me?" he asked once we reached the house.

"I'd love to," I said, and followed him inside. "I used to watch films with Marjorie. Videos seem to have died out – they're all on CDs these days, aren't they?"

Oliver rolled his eyes. "DVDs, or Blu-rays, but I stream most of mine. It means I can just click on a title and we can watch it. What sort of thing do you like?"

"I doubt we've got the same taste; I love romantic stuff. My favourite film was *Edward Scissorhands*."

"Let's see if it's on Netflix." He pointed a tiny remote control at the screen and scrolled through a bewildering array of options on the screen. "No, sorry, I'll get it for you next time. But tonight, let's see. I know, *Harry Potter*. Think you'll like it."

"You sure you want to stay in, just on my account? It's Saturday night."

"This is what I normally do." He rubbed his nose. "I guess

I'd better 'fess up. You'll work it out soon, Rowena, but I'm a bit of a saddo."

I frowned, not recognising the expression.

"Geek, dork, nerd, whatever they called them back in the nineties. You know, people who aren't cool. People who are more happy in cyberspace than reality." He rolled his eyes. "That means playing on the computer. It's the equivalent of sitting in, reading or listening to gramophone records or whatever they did in your day."

I smiled. "I don't believe you. I don't think there's anything sad about you."

"You'd be surprised. Can't remember when I was last out on a Saturday night."

"What a waste. There I was, dying to go out clubbing on a Saturday night, but no-one ever asked me because of my face, and there's you, a good-looking guy, choosing not to. Can't we go to a club?"

"Yeah, I'm going to look a right spaz, aren't I, dancing on my own." He shrugged. "Were people always so cruel about the way you looked? Didn't you ever go out? Do normal teenage stuff'

"Not much. Never even been drunk. Had a couple of ciders with some of my friends from the day centre, one especially, Kirsty, but she couldn't go out because she had a blood disease and the drugs she took buggered up her immune system. She died, about a year after me. It was a funny mix, that centre. They were all normal teenagers – moody, hormonal, horny – but the rest of the world thought that because they were disabled, that they didn't feel what other people felt. Every now and again we'd go round each other's houses but it had to be planned ages in advance because most of them needed their folks or carers to transport them. We could never be spontaneous. And even most of them didn't fancy me. No-one did."

"I would have." I loved that wink. "But y'know what? If we'd met in real life, I wouldn't be able to speak to you. I get tongue-tied if a girl comes near me. I can hardly string a sentence together."

"You're doing all right with me." Then I realised he wasn't joking. "God, really? What do you think made you that way?"

"I dunno. My mum and endless bloody 'uncles' didn't help. The world I created inside my head was always kind of better than real life. And by the time I had to go to school, interact with other people, I just hadn't learned how to do it, y'know? They don't teach you that at school, do they? And of course there was my hair."

"But you said the bullying stopped as you got older?"

"Yeah, but by then the damage was done. Other kids had a natural confidence. Not me. And in my first school report I was labelled, and that was that. 'Shy'." He spat the word, his mouth turning down as if it tasted bad in his mouth.

"Is that such a bad thing?"

"Hell, yeah. It's impossible to understand unless you've been shy yourself. Your whole personality becomes encapsulated in one word, and no-one makes the effort to get to know you. Huh, shy. The epitaph for the terminally insignificant. When I die, they'll probably carve it on my gravestone."

"And when you got to university, it didn't improve?"

"A little. I have a few mates. But fresher's week – it's like the first day of school multiplied by a thousand. Everyone's putting themselves out there – trying to collect as many friends as possible – and I'm just one of those guys who doesn't make a good first impression. Not to mention the fact that I'm younger than the rest of them – I was still seventeen back then. I didn't have any trouble getting served in pubs because of my height but it makes a difference, y'know." He sighed. "I'm self-conscious about every little thing I say or do."

To be honest, I didn't know what to say to him. I hadn't got that impression at all. I'd seen him in the phone shop and heard him talking to the police. He'd sounded so sure of himself.

"So sad," I said, which I don't suppose helped much. "And you have no reason to be. But you could look after yourself more. Starting with a haircut."

"What's wrong with my hair?"

"There's something called a comb. Ever used one?"

He grinned. "This from the girl who always shows up in a jumper with holes in the sleeves. You never found it difficult to talk to people?"

"Not difficult as such, but I got used to not making an effort with new people. It was a kind of armour: reject them before they rejected me."

"Perhaps that's why we connect so well. Because neither of us felt part of this world."

"Tell you what." I grinned. "Let's go clubbing in here."

Oliver selected a playlist on his tablet and together we started moving to the music. You have to remember that dancing was a new experience for me, and at first I mirrored Oliver's movements, unsure what to do, but soon it became natural. And then we didn't care, grinning like idiots, happy and alive. It was as if my true self had come out to play for the first time and all there was in the world was Oliver, me, the beat of the music and the freedom to be whoever the hell I liked. I couldn't wipe the smile from my face, and it wasn't just the dancing. It was the knowledge that I'd finally found a kindred spirit and for as long as Oliver formed part of my reality, I'd no longer feel lonely.

CHAPTER 10

14th April 2014

I nuzzled closer to Oliver as the closing titles played. About halfway through *Harry Potter and the Philosopher's Stone*, he'd put his arm around me and I'd rested my head against him. I could feel his heartbeat, even his warmth. It was hard to concentrate on the film.

"That was fantastic," I said. "And there's a whole series of these?"

"Yeah. We can watch another tomorrow if you like."

"I'd love to. I can't remember when I've ever enjoyed an evening like this."

"Me neither."

My nose wrinkled. "I can smell the beer on your breath!"

"Why shouldn't you? You said before that you can smell me."

"It's so strange. I can almost taste it."

"Perhaps you can taste through me." He grinned. "I'll breathe on you every time I eat from now on, especially after garlic bread."

I moved closer to take in his breath once more. But being so close to his mouth unsettled me. What would his lips feel like against mine? The overpowering urge to find out made me feel so faint that I moved away. He rubbed his nose, straightened his body and turned to pick up his tablet.

"Shall we check the news, see if there's anything about Jasmine?" He looked at the screen then gasped. "Oh my God, look."

The headline read: *JASMINE: MAN HELD. A man is being questioned in relation to the disappearance of Jasmine Fletcher.*

"Wow, they took you seriously. That was quick. I'd better

go back to Hampstead Heath, try and find Jasmine and tell her the good news."

With the hyperspeed I could now reach without a second thought, I soon found myself at the top of Parliament Hill. Damn, no sign of Jasmine. Then I saw Frank, walking with a woman wearing a red velvet dress and black hooded cloak. Honestly, she looked like a cross between a goth and the Wicked Witch of the West. I shouted and waved at them.

"Hello, love. Thought you'd be back," Frank grinned. "Rowena, meet Alice."

"Hi Rowena," Alice said then turned to Frank. "She's the one you told me about?"

"Aye, this is her," he said.

"Ah, she has an incredible aura," the woman said.

Aura? Seriously? She'd be talking about chakras next. I remember some of the quacks that used to give false hope to Kirsty's parents when things were looking bleak with her illness; as if three sugar tablets and a glass of wheatgrass juice was going to make her bone marrow produce blood cells again. It had made me cynical about all things 'alternative'. But this must be the woman who might be able give me some answers. Talk about bad timing; I needed to find Jasmine as soon as possible. "Hi, are you going to be here long? I'd love to talk to you, but right now I'm on an urgent mission. I was looking for a girl around my age. Her name's Jasmine. I've got to tell her something."

"Jasmine? Don't think I know her," said Frank.

"She hasn't been here long. She was murdered. I think I may have done what she needs, to pass over. Oh hell, where is she? Do ghosts always go to sleep where they're buried?"

"We prefer to be called spirits," said Alice. Ugh, she was so up herself. How badly did I want answers from her?

"Ignore her," said Frank. "Political correctness – load of old shite if you ask me. A ghost's a ghost. But yeah, where did you think you went to sleep?"

"I've never thought about it," I said. So I must be transported to Suffolk when time passed in my absence. How strange that I had no awareness of it. "I'd better go to Queen's Wood then. That's where her body is."

"Can we come?" Alice said. "I've never seen anyone pass

over. You can tell me all about yourself afterwards."

"Sure." I frowned. I was becoming less impressed with Alice by the minute. It seemed distasteful to watch someone passing if you had no connection to them.

Frank rolled his eyes. "It's not a sodding sideshow," he snarled, then turned to me. "Bloody tourist, this one. That's why she's here."

"Sorry?" I said.

"I chose to come here, to finish my research," said Alice.

"She means she topped herself." Frank sniffed.

A million childhood flashbacks from church and school hit me. Suicide was a sin. Shouldn't Alice be in hell by now?

"I liberated myself from the earthly realm." Alice gave a haughty tilt of the chin. I resisted the urge to slap her. Still, if this was what it took to get some insight into that last few days, I'd put up with her pretentious claptrap.

"You chucked yourself off the top of the Lloyds building." Frank turned to me. "Don't ever look under her hood; half her brains are bashed in."

"I remember seeing that on the news," I said. So Alice had kept her injuries. I remembered Frank's comment about inner beauty and couldn't resist a smug smile.

"It was symbolic," said Alice. "A rejection of capitalism. I'd had enough of that world – ghastly place. I never did belong there. All my life I'd been interested in the paranormal – I spent years researching it. I chose to join that dimension."

Frank rolled his eyes and winked. I winked back. Give me down to earth Frank any day rather than this woman who seemed to have had a sense of humour bypass.

"But how could you know you'd return as a ghost ... sorry, spirit?" I asked "What if you'd just passed over?"

"I was more spiritual than the average person. I guess I was able to choose."

Frank gave a sound that was half snort, half sniff. Luckily there wasn't a chance for me to comment, as the wood was coming into view. And then I saw something else. The entrance was closed off by police tape and floodlights lit up the whole wood. I rushed through the tape and soon found the search party. But they were looking in the wrong place.

Jasmine, a good fifty metres away, was frantically waving and shouting.

"Rowena!" she said. "Was this you?"

"Yeah, my friend called the police. They've got your boyfriend. Why are they looking over there?"

"They set off on the wrong path. I keep trying to attract their attention but no-one's taking any notice."

"It's easy, watch," said Frank. "I used to do this for a laugh."

He picked up a handful of leaves and twigs and let them fall, but it didn't make enough the noise to attract the attention of the men.

I shrugged. "I can't do that."

Jasmine and Alice reached to the ground but their hands passed straight through the leaves. Oh good, it wasn't just me.

"Women. No bloody practical skills," Frank said. "Leave it to me."

He tossed a bigger armful of twigs and leaves in the air.

"What was that?" The men turned their torches in our direction and the dog that was with them started to bark. The dog handler released it. It bounded towards us, barking ferociously.

"Hey, calm down, lad," said Frank, and scratched the dog behind the ear. I tried, but failed. The dog wagged its tail but had now picked up the scent of Jasmine's body. It barked once more, scratching at the raised mound.

"Over here, guys," shouted the dog handler and soon the men were rummaging through the makeshift grave.

Even though I was expecting it, I jumped a mile, as did the policemen, when Jasmine's arm popped out of the earth. Soon they'd uncovered her face, her eyes bloated and her tongue protruding. It was hard to believe that this hideous corpse had belonged to the stunning girl standing next to me. Judging by the gagging noises of the policemen, she didn't small too good either.

"Looks like her, all right. Seal off the area; I'll call in forensics. Call the station, Phil. Let's see if we can get that toerag Johnson talking."

"Fuck, that's me. It's really me." Jasmine gasped. "Think

I'm gonna hurl."

"Come away; you've done what you needed to do." I took her arm and led her away, Frank and Alice following.

"Thanks, babes. I dunno what to say," said Jasmine.

"I-I guess it should be over for you soon." I drew Jasmine towards me for a hug and then gasped – my arm had begun to sink into Jasmine's back.

"Wow, this is awesome!" said Jasmine, and her face lit up into same blissful expression I'd seen on Marjorie. Whatever that next life involved, it seemed to be a happy place.

When we pulled apart, Jasmine's hands were no longer there. Her body was dissolving in front of us. It only took around thirty seconds, and then she'd completely disappeared, leaving nothing but the barely visible glow that I'd seen when Marjorie passed.

"Goodbye, Jasmine," I whispered.

"Wow! That was breathtaking," said Alice, as if she'd been watching a firework display.

"Show a bit of respect can't you?" said Frank. "We should have a minute's silence."

We stood in a semicircle around where Jasmine had been. Frank put his hand on my shoulder. How bizarre, already I felt part of this community of ghosts and for so long I didn't even know it existed. As we walked away, Alice turned to me.

"Frank told me all about you," she said. "And you sound like you have a fascinating story."

"I guess so …" I wasn't sure I wanted to tell Alice; I doubted she had any genuine insights.

"So let me get this straight. There's only one person who sees and hear you, and he can touch you?"

"That's right. Oliver. I snuggled up against him this evening while we watched a film. I could feel everything, his warmth, his heart beating." At the thought of him, I smiled. "I could even smell him. And he could feel me, except for the heartbeat."

"And he was born on the day you died?"

I nodded.

"So he's the reason you're here, not his grandmother. She was the vessel to lead you to him. I wonder … I think that when people die unexpectedly, sometimes they touch the soul of someone that's special to them. But in your case it seems more than that, as if you left a piece of yourself behind. Perhaps when you died, part of your soul went into Oliver."

Frank tossed his head. "Sounds like a load of old shite to me."

"But he wasn't special to me. I hadn't even met him at that stage. Besides, he was born about twelve hours before I died. He was in a hospital five miles away. Why would I give him a piece of my soul?"

"You tell me. How do you feel about Oliver? I mean, imagine if you were alive and you'd met him under normal circumstances."

I took a deep breath. "Even when he was a little boy, I felt a special connection to him. I had these maternal impulses that I'd never had when I was alive. But now I feel like … he's the man of my dreams. It's like we look at life the same way."

"Bloody hell, you didn't tell me that." Frank shook his head.

"Oh my God, you're soul mates," Alice said, with enough drama to send Frank's eyes rolling skyward.

"Well yeah, I guess so."

"No, you're not getting my meaning," said Alice with the exaggerated patience that adults use when explaining something to a small child. "People in the earthly dimension overuse the phrase, cheapen it. True soul mates are a rare thing. Sometimes a soul splits in two and goes into two bodies. The two souls are destined to keep meeting each other over and over."

"What, you mean like in reincarnation?" I frowned. How could Alice know this for sure?

"Well yes, obviously. It seems that you and Oliver have been separated in time. That's why the two of you are so real to each other."

"She's making it up as she goes along," said Frank.

But it made perfect sense to me. Look how many experiences we shared – unwanted children, mothers dying of cancer when we were sixteen. That feeling, even when he was a baby, that I knew him already. And – let's face it – it sounded so romantic, I wanted to believe it. I looked at Alice with new eyes. This was a story I could completely buy into.

"How romantic," said Alice. "I think you've been waiting for him. The only way you can pass over is with him."

"Looks like you're sticking around for a while then," said Frank. "He could be alive for sixty years yet."

"That's up to Rowena," Alice said. "Only she can decide."

"I don't see how I've got a choice," I said. "Every time I try to leave, I get pulled back."

"There might be another way. Frank said that you'd never been kissed."

"Yeah. Pathetic, eh?"

"But if you kiss him, you've connected in this incarnation. That might be all it takes. Of course; that's it! You'll be able to pass over then."

I put my hands to my lips.

"I almost kissed him this evening, but I stopped because I felt like I was about to pass out. That's happened every time I get close to him."

"Because every time you get close to making that connection, you get close to releasing yourself. It's your choice," said Alice. Then without warning, she clutched her chest, writhed in pain, and disappeared.

Frank shrugged. "That happens every time I see her," he said. "The lass says some things that make you think, but she's about as spiritual as my arse. Suicides, seen 'em before. Not sure I know much about souls, but I reckon something inside them breaks. Tortured, the lot of them. They don't settle anywhere."

The thought of it gave me the shivers. "Horrible. Interesting though ... what she said about Oliver. Do you think there was any truth in it?

"Search me, love," said Frank. "All sounded a bit fanciful for my liking. Might be worth a try though. Give the lad a smacker; set yourself free."

I could, couldn't I? But was I ready to go?

CHAPTER 11

15th April 2014

I found Oliver in front of the TV.

"Be careful," he said. "The paint on that wall's still wet. Huh, what am I saying? Like you need to worry."

I placed my palm to the wall and held it up to him, clean.

"She's on the news, look," he said.

Jasmine's photo was on the telly. Underneath a banner headline read: *JASMINE: BODY FOUND. Boyfriend arrested on suspicion of murder.* Jasmine's mother appeared on the screen, sobbing.

"So you did it," Oliver said. "That's awesome."

"It was an incredible night." I told him every detail. "I wish you could have been there, when Jasmine passed over. It was so beautiful, just like it was for your nan. I wondered if it'd be different for her, because she'd died violently."

"Hey, don't get any ideas." Oliver put his hand over mine. "You're not going anywhere. I need you to help me choose some furniture, then we can watch another *Harry Potter* film."

There, he'd made the decision, not me. My mind had been churning. Should I share Alice's theories with him? They made sense last night but today they seemed whimsical, crackpot even. But twin soul or not, he wanted me around. What harm could it do? Didn't I deserve a little enjoyment?

"Sounds good," I said. "Can I choose anything I like?"

"Anything. Turns out that Nan had quite a bit in savings. I'm pretty well off. I've bookmarked some online stores."

"You can even go shopping on this thing? You'd never need to leave the house!"

We spent the morning flicking screens that displayed all manner of furniture: modern or retro, rustic or plastic, and I fantasised that we were married. Then I snapped myself out of it and I decided that Oliver should have a proper single guy's paradise: metal-framed black and white photos, black leather sofas, and a massive flat-screen telly with surround sound.

Sometimes I adored my existence: I skipped all boring bits of a life and turned up for the interesting parts, like fast-forwarding over the dull parts of a film. When I next materialised, Oliver was sitting on the new sofa in front of an enormous futuristic-looking telly.

"Bloody hell, I've seen cinema screens smaller than that." I said.

"Trust you to turn up now all the hard work's done."

"Wow!" I took it all in. "And you've had your hair cut. It's really cool."

"Thought I'd better blend in with the room." He put his hand to his hair, which was stunning – tapered in at the back and sides, with the top long enough to fall across his forehead. He was wearing new clothes too – black jeans and long-sleeved T-shirt – simple and stylish. He wasn't even slouching any more. A horror thought struck me – had he met a girl?

"This isn't just a haircut; it's a whole new image. Trying to impress someone, are you?"

"Yeah. You. So, what d'you reckon? All OK for you?"

I glowed. The new look was for me? "Almost. We could make it more cosy though. A few cushions, perhaps?"

"What is it with girls and cushions?" He grinned. "Go on then. Any particular colour?"

"Something bright would work in here. Fuchsia pink and violet, perhaps."

Oliver shook his head, smiling. "Let's have a look online. He tapped on his screen, again and searched for a minute. How would these suit madam?"

"Mmm, perfect."

He clicked on the screen

"There you go. They're all yours. They should be delivered in a few days."

"I love the internet!" I said. "Have you done that playlist yet?"

"Finished it last night."

I'd asked Oliver to made a playlist of the music that had been the soundtrack to his life so far, and we settled into our favourite topic of conversation. At the third track, something I'd never heard before, I fell silent. The powerful music moved me like nothing I'd ever heard before.

"What's this?" I said softly.

"A band called Elbow. Beautiful, isn't it?"

He drew closer, so close that our noses were almost touching. I gazed into his eyes and felt the warmth of his breath. Time slowed down, I swear. Mills and Boon overload. This was every romantic cliché I'd ever read. Then, it was as if something snapped inside me, sending me back to a place of sanity. If Alice's theory was right, this could be the moment that completed my journey and then I'd be gone from here forever. How could I take that risk? I moved my face away so Oliver's lips made contact with my cheek instead.

"Sorry, but we can't," I mumbled.

Oliver cupped my face in his hands. "Why not? I don't care that you're not … real. You are to me, so that's all that matters, surely? I've never felt like this about anyone before, let alone being able to express it in words. But with you, it's easy." His eyes dipped and then met mine again. "I love you. There, I said it. I can't fight it any more than I can fight gravity. For most of my life I've daydreamed about you in one form or other. As a kid I wanted you to be my mum, then when I hit my teens, it was a completely different sort of fantasy. And now I want to spend every minute of the day with you. You're the first person I think of every morning and the last person I see at night."

I closed my eyes, to let the impact of his words sink in. My thoughts blurred and I had to grip his arm, needing something to anchor me to the earth. It took every shred of my willpower, but I forced myself to stay in the present. It was almost a minute before I could speak.

"I love you too, Oliver. I've loved you from the minute I saw you. Being with you is like finally coming home. But we can't risk kissing. It's going to sound bonkers but I met a ghost the night Jasmine passed. She seemed to make sense of

… me and you. She thinks we're true soul mates. That a soul split and went into two bodies. She thinks we've met in past lives."

I noticed his eyes glaze over in the way cynics do when listening to something they clearly think is bullshit. He didn't speak for a while, as if processing the information. Then he grinned.

"I don't believe in all that crap, but I know we're meant to be together." He clasped my hands. "When I'm with you I feel complete. You must have noticed that I don't stammer when I'm with you?"

"Yeah, but I assumed you'd just grown out of it."

"No … I still do. But not when we went to the mobile phone shop, or when I was talking to the police. That's why I put on the accent; for some reason I don't stammer when I imitate other people. But I reckon that I'd have been OK, anyway. It's because you were with me. I need you, you see."

"I need you, too. I need to experience some of the things I was meant to experience in life. Oliver … the more I think about it, the more I think Alice was right." I told him every detail of the evening, becoming more convinced of the theory with every word I said. "We were separated in time. The timing of births and deaths can be so random."

"I want to believe it," he said. "But it sounds like this woman's full of shit."

"She is, to be honest. There's so much we don't understand, that's the problem. Spirits might need to rest between incarnations. We know from my experience that when you're dead, time doesn't go in a straight line. I've missed the last two weeks. I skipped three years after you were sixteen. Some kids sleep for decades."

"We're never gonna know the truth, are we? But none of this explains why we can't kiss." He raised an eyebrow, making me grin. I loved flirty Oliver. "If we can experience each other physically, we should take full advantage of it."

"Well … Alice thinks there are only two ways I can pass. I can either wait for you, or I can kiss you. That way we'll have made the connection we need in this lifetime."

"Sounds like a fairytale to me, and not in a good way." He frowned. "Why a kiss?"

"You see." I reached for a strand of hair. "For me, the kiss is the ultimate fantasy. Ever since I was ten, I dreamed of this big moment. It's a huge thing for me. And there have been times in the last few weeks, when my feelings have become too overwhelming, that I've become faint, as if I'm about to leave you. And I couldn't stand that."

"Neither could I." He stroked my face and I closed my eyes. His fingertips touched my eyelids, soft like feathers. Wow. No-one had ever touched my eyelids. When I opened them, I saw a dreamy expression on his face – his eyes soft, his lips parted. I placed my fingers to them, felt their fullness, and smoothed away the groove between his eyebrows.

"No kisses it is, then," he said. "Ah well, I'm better off than Edward Scissorhands. At least I get to hold you."

"Sorry, sweetheart," I said, "Pretty bum deal for you, isn't it?"

"You were the only person who ever called me sweetheart." He smiled. "Makes me feel about six."

"Oh shit, sorry. Maybe it's not the right thing to call you any more."

"No, I love it," he said. "Maybe we could just have a slow dance. This was my mum's favourite record. I always wanted to dance to it with someone special."

The sounds of a beautiful song filled the room. Who'd have thought bitch Sarah had such good taste in music? At the words "You do something to me," he stood and held out his hand. At first he held me carefully, like I was a fragile object that might break. But as he moved in time to the music, he drew me closer. I buried my head into his shoulder, closed my eyes and sank into an ecstatic haze. I felt every detail of him, the softness of his cotton shirt, the faint sheen of sweat on his skin, the hardness of his belt buckle and below, a kind of disconcerting hardness on which I didn't dwell.

And if, deep down, I knew I was existing on borrowed time, I pushed the thought aside. Just for once, why shouldn't I live the dream?

CHAPTER 12

9th June 2014

"Oliver, the sun's out!"

"Finally! I was beginning to think I'd cursed the whole summer." Oliver had blown some of his inheritance on an open-top sports car. Since then, it had rained every weekend, but today the blue skies glowed with the promise that only early summer could bring. "How about a proper day out, away from London, I mean? Maybe the coast."

"That'd be amazing. But I haven't been away from London before, apart from my funeral. Whenever I try to go too far, I get pulled back."

"But that was before me. Let's try it. If you disappear, I'll go back home. Where do you fancy?"

He was right, you see. Things had changed. I'd been existing in real time more in April and May than I had in the last five years. I disappeared every night but rematerialised each time Oliver was at home.

"How about Suffolk? We could get there in two hours. There are some lovely beaches. And ... it sounds weird, but I'd like to see my grave. My home village was by the sea."

"Sounds good," he said, kissing my forehead.

Oh yes, that's another thing. We'd discovered that quite a lot of kissing was safe; we just hadn't tried lip-to-lip contact. We'd been pushing the boundaries, Oliver pulling away if I showed any sort of sign that I might be about to fade away. And to say I was happy would be the biggest understatement in the world. I was ecstatic. I know how vomit-inducing this sounds, but being with Oliver was an absolute joy. Every boring domestic task – from watching him iron his shirt to emptying the dishwasher – had turned into something special.

Still, I was nervous when I got into the car with him. We

left the safe streets of Muswell Hill and headed towards the North Circular, where all was cars and noise. But within half an hour we'd left the traffic-clogged roads of London behind and were speeding along the motorway. And I didn't feel the least bit dizzy; in fact I was buzzing. I leaned over to touch his hair, which was blowing chaotically around his face.

"I've never driven in an open-top car before. I feel like a film star!" I shouted.

"You look like one." He smiled. "Except for the fact that your hair doesn't move, and no film star ever dressed like that."

I glanced at my slippers and laughed. We'd given up trying to make sense of my physicality. Sometimes I could swear my heart was pounding, even though I knew it wasn't possible. We'd concluded that Frank was partially right – a spirit feels what they expect to feel – but in my case I felt what I wanted to feel. Today I felt the wind against my cheek and yet it wasn't moving my hair.

Once we reached the quieter roads of Suffolk, I smiled.

"This is going to be such a nostalgia-fest. Gorgeous, isn't it? I always felt the sky was bigger here than everywhere else."

"It is. You can see forever can't you? And we've been driving – let's see – an hour and a half and you haven't disappeared."

"I feel absolutely fine. No, better than that. I feel like I'm finally living."

"Me too. When I'm with you, I get this crazy feeling, like we can do anything. Hey, you know what this means? We can go away together, places I've always wanted to see. Paris. Rome. The Grand Canyon. We could go skiing."

"Sounds like heaven. I've never even been on a plane," I said, and that's how we were for the rest of the journey – a fantasy travelogue. Then I saw it.

"Hey, you've gone quiet. What's up?"

"See that church in the distance? That's where I'm buried."

"We'd better have a look for your grave then, hadn't we?"

The graveyard was tiny compared to the ones in Highgate and Finchley, and there was no-one sleeping by the graves. In fact, the only signs of anything ever having been alive here was the dead rabbit under a yew tree. Most of the graves were untended and unloved. The grass was overgrown around some of the stones, almost obliterating them from existence. It took us a while to locate my gravestone, and when we did, Oliver took my hand in his. It was a plain, puny stone, probably the cheapest in the catalogue. And it was splattered with lichens and moss, hammering home just how long I'd been dead.

"Rowena Hill, died 1995, age 19 years. Beloved daughter of Kathleen and Edward." Oliver read the inscription on the simple headstone, with a shaky voice. "You really did die. I can go weeks without remembering."

"Hey, you've got my soul. It's worth a hell of a lot more than my body."

"But I want you all," he muttered, and for the first time I detected bitterness in his voice.

When I spoke it was to change the uncomfortable subject. "I think this is where I go when I disappear. Frank said that's what happens to ghosts. I was never sure, but now I am. I think I sleep there" – I pointed to a patch of grass under a tree close to my grave. "It feels familiar."

"Doesn't look as comfortable as my bed." He grinned.

"Don't start that again. I can't risk it, can I? Course I'd love to sleep with you, but what if I never wake up?" I swear his eyes had darkened with disappointment, and it wasn't just a wave of panic flooding over me; it was a tsunami. What we had wasn't enough for him. I guess it was bound to happen. But what would happen to me when he'd had enough of playing with ghosts and found himself a real life girlfriend?

"Are they your parents?" He looked towards the larger stones next to mine.

"Yes. Oh look, my Dad died years ago." The stone was inscribed with the words: Here lies Edward Hill, died 2001, age 73 years, and also his wife Kathleen Hill, died 1992, age 63 years. But the memory of them only brought mild sadness and nostalgia. No-one, not even Marjorie, had touched me in life the way Oliver had in death.

Oliver turned away and bent to the ground. At first I thought he was upset, then I noticed that he was picking buttercups. I watched him collect a bunch, then place them at the foot of my gravestone.

"Someone should leave you flowers," he said.

A cloud momentarily took the sun away. Perhaps it hadn't been a good idea to come here.

"Let's go to the beach," I said. "If we head north from the village it's usually deserted."

The idea raised both our spirits, and we raced each other across the sand dunes to the sea. Apart from a handful of families, the beach was quiet and a five-minute walk gave us a stretch of sand, shielded by wooden sea defences, that was entirely ours. The sea was inviting, not even a slight breeze to stir its surface. As a kid, I used to imagine that this beach belonged to me, the sea was my own personal paddling pool. Now it seemed like the backdrop to a romantic film, and finally I was the star.

"Come on, let's go in!" he said.

He took off his trainers and pulled the T-shirt over his head then undid his jeans, stripping down to his boxer shorts. I stared at his naked chest, and the most peculiar feeling came over me. He was broader than I'd expected, his flesh milky-white, his chest hairless except for a few pale hairs that curled around his nipples.

"Tell me you're going to take that sweater off," he said.

I looked downwards – I hadn't removed these clothes in nineteen years – did they even come off? But they did. And what was I wearing underneath? Oh, thank God. My matching lilac bra and pants.

"That's a relief. I *was* wearing my best underwear. It's been so long that I'd forgotten."

"God, you're beautiful," he said in a way that made me feel all-powerful and uneasy at the same time.

He picked me up – we'd already discovered that I weighed about four stones in his arms – he was aware of my weight but I was nowhere near as heavy as I should be – and plunged into the sea.

"Bloody hell, it's freezing!" he said.

"Is it? I can't feel it." I couldn't feel anything – no wetness, no chill.

"I'll make you feel it."

He waded deeper and flung me in. But I sank to the bottom and didn't float back. To me, the water had no more substance than the walls I passed through. I sat there, in a state of disbelief, on the ribbed sand of the seabed. My hands looked white and as if they didn't belong to me. Oliver's hand reached for mine and yanked me upright.

"Forgot you can't breathe." He grinned. "For a second I thought you'd drowned. But that was so cool. You really sat on the seabed?"

"I suppose so. I was hoping to feel the sea, though." I touched my hair. And look – I'm perfectly dry."

"Crazy, isn't it. Guess you can't swim, either?"

I tried to launch myself into the water, but my body refused to co-operate. I waded out again, seething with jealousy as Oliver's arms sliced through the water.

"I so wanted to swim. Sometimes I hate being a ghost," I said, when he came out.

"Come here. I think you're a bloody miracle." He drew me towards him.

"Don't kiss me!"

"Sorry. It's hard not to."

And then I smelt something familiar.

"You smell of the sea." I grinned. "I used to breathe in great lungfuls of salty air when I visited here, like I was flushing London's polluted air out of my system, but I can't smell it, except on your skin. Isn't that the strangest thing?"

"Can you taste it?" he asked.

He placed a finger to my lips. I opened my mouth and he inserted the finger. And I tasted it! The sharp tang of salt on my tongue! I tightened my lips around his finger, lost in the long-forgotten sensation of taste. He removed his finger and inserted each one in turn. It wasn't until I looked at his face, his lips parted, his breathing quickened, that I realised what I was doing.

"Let's sit down," he said.

We sat at the water's edge, and I placed my head against his chest, neither of us able to put words to the strange intimacy we'd just shared. And now I was feeling a new bodily sensation – one I'd never felt in life – like a fire burning low down inside me. Which didn't make sense, when you thought about it. All the other bodily sensations I'd felt could be explained as remembered feelings – my ghost feels what it expects to feel. But Frank's crack about me being a convent girl had been embarrassingly close to the truth. My fantasies had never got further than kissing a man and now I cursed my naivety. After the accident, I'd been excluded from the normal teen gossip and speculation about sex, as if everyone assumed it was something I'd never experience. I'd read about it in books of course; I understood the basics. But the average twelve year-old was probably more clued up than me.

"Are you OK?" Oliver broke the silence.

"Yeah, just ..."

"Intense. I know," he said. "Let's just lie here for now. I'd better put some more sunscreen on. I always fry in the sun. Could you do my back?"

I moved behind him, and placed my hands onto a patch of skin, shiny with sunscreen, between his shoulder blades, feeling the heat of the sun on his skin. It took me a while to get the hang of spreading the lotion – at first my fingers passed straight through a thick white blob, but as my hands moved in slow circles over his back, the sunscreen dispersed. And again, I lost myself, exploring every bone and muscle, as if the living flesh under my hands might bring me back to life. It was only when I heard him give a soft moan that I stopped.

"We shouldn't be doing this, should we?" I said. "I'm teasing you."

"I'll take my thrills any way I can." He laughed. "Can I do the same to you? I know you're not going to get burnt, but indulge me."

"OK." I let him trace slow, sensuous circles on my back, and for a few minutes the feeling I experienced was the closest to bliss I'd ever been, but then the faintness started.

"Sorry, I'm fading. You'd better stop."

We lay on the sand, and I draped my hand across his chest.

"This is more like it. I can't feel the heat of the sun on my own body, but I can feel it on yours."

We lay there, in safer territory, for ages, but eventually a couple with a dog shattered our idyll.

"I guess we were never going to have the place to ourselves on a day like this," Oliver said.

"Don't talk! Imagine how you'll look to them, a mental case, talking to yourself. Let's head away – look, the dog's seen me. It's going nuts already."

A border collie started barking and circling us, much to the embarrassment of the apologetic owners.

"OK, I'm hungry anyway."

I picked up my clothes. For one glorious, decadent moment, I wondered what it would be like to spend the rest of my existence wearing only my underwear. But, judging by the effect it had on Oliver, it probably wouldn't be fair. I put on the slippers, jumper and leggings.

As we returned to the village I tried to shake the cloud that had started to gather above my head. So far our trips to the outside world had been places where we could be together inconspicuously – the cinema, theatre and concerts. Today should have been a paradise – and parts of it had been – but at the same time it was showcasing all the things I couldn't do. To tell you the truth, I felt like giving up and going home, but I knew I should put on a show of cheerfulness for Oliver's sake.

"What do you want to do about lunch?" I asked, "There's a lovely thatched pub, but being with me in public might be not be much fun for you."

I saw the shadow pass over his face and knew that he was sharing my doubts about the success of the day.

"Who cares? Let's go anyway. It's a perfect day to sit in a pub garden."

And so we found ourselves facing each other across a wooden table. I watched with envy as the barmaid laid a plate of scampi, salad and chips in front of Oliver. Was there a look of pity in her eye? Oliver had seen it too. He shuffled in his seat, clearly uncomfortable at the image he thought other people saw: Billy no-mates, eating out alone. I kept up the one-sided conversation I'd started since we sat down, but it was becoming harder and harder to stay upbeat.

"That looks fantastic. Scampi was always my favourite. If I was drinking I'd have … let's see … one of those." I pointed to a glass of Pimms on the next table. "It looks like summer in a glass. Oh, I wish we would make the world go away so we could have all this to ourselves."

He smiled but that frown line between his eyes had appeared.

"This isn't good for you, is it?" I said softly

He made an attempt at a smile but shook his head.

"Feel like everyone's looking at you and wondering why you're here on your own?"

He nodded.

"I know how that feels. I used to feel that people were giving me pitying looks wherever I went. Mind you, in my case I was usually right. They'd be pretending not to look at me, but at the same time they had a morbid fascination with my face. Invisibility worked out well for me. But as for you, I reckon no-one's paying you the slightest bit of attention. Remember me telling you how I used to spy on people in public places?" He raised an eyebrow. "One thing I learned is that no-one makes judgement on people being on their own. Watch this."

I walked around each of the tables in the garden, had a quick listen in on each conversation, and reported back.

"That couple over there don't like each other's company. The woman's checking her mobile under the table. That woman's keeping an eye on her dog. The dog's got his eye on the cat that's asleep on the wall. And those two" – I pointed at two unsmiling women at the neighbouring table – "are breaking up with each other. Not one person is saying, look at that guy on his own."

"Thanks," he mouthed but I could tell he wasn't convinced.

"What are we doing, Oliver? I'm the world's worst girlfriend." I muttered.

He grabbed my hand.

"You know what? I don't care." This time he spoke aloud, and some heads turned. "When it's just you and me, I can be the person I want to be. I can be funny and charming and confident. Then I go back to real life and I'm the shy, geeky kid with the stammer. So let's keep it as you and me."

"You and me it is. There are plenty of deserted places we can be together. Who needs other people?"

We left for home after that, both of us keeping up a sense of forced cheerfulness, like those trying to deal with bad news. And even then, deep down, I knew it was wrong.

Oliver needed other people.

CHAPTER 13

3rd September, 2014

I materialised in the living room one evening, and noticed that Oliver was wearing a different shirt.

"How long was I gone?" I asked.

"Only two days." Oliver kissed my cheek. "Don't look so guilty. I can cope, you know."

I buried myself into his chest. It had been a while since I'd had a two-day break from him. Never before had my time scale been so close to that of the living.

"See, I can last a week on that," he said. "Fancy an orange?"

I nodded. It was our favourite game. Slowly, deliberately, he peeled the fruit, letting the tiny explosions of zest fall on his hands. He slowed his pace, teasing me. I honestly felt like my mouth was watering. He separated each segment, eating them slowly. Seeing the juice on his lips, I had to look away for a moment. When he'd finished eating, he held out his hand. I sucked his fingertips then licked the juice from his palms. That combination of sweetness and acidity was the best flavour in the world. Funny to think that when I was alive I used to eat my microwave dinners mechanically, without paying any attention to their flavour. When you've been deprived of any sort of sensory pleasure, you learn to savour it.

As the taste faded, I traced the lines of his hands with my tongue and then moved away. This was the awkward part. I burned with the pleasure of it all, but also with the guilt of knowing that it should be leading up to something more, something I couldn't give him. Then came the fear. Fear that we'd taken it too far, that I'd be taken from him.

"Was it good for you too?" he joked.

"Incredible. You give good orange." This was our coping strategy. We had to normalise it, to make ourselves believe that our relationship was the same as anyone else's.

But I didn't just have Oliver, these days. My afterlife had never been so full. I'd met no end of new friends, but I couldn't share them with Oliver. They were all ghosts. That night, I made one of my now-regular trips to the Heath. But tonight I had a special reason for the visit.

"Hi, Christine," I said, smiling at the thirtysomething mum who'd been electrocuted, but met her young children after school every day.

"Rowena, hi," she said. "Did Alice invite you here?"

"Yeah, but I don't know why." I shrugged. "Do you?"

"Not a clue. She said she wanted all her friends here. Perhaps it's her birthday." Christine laughed.

We reached the top of Parliament Hill – wow – I'd never seen so many ghouls together in one place, then caught sight of Frank. I hadn't seen him for most of the summer.

"Hi Frank. What's this all about?"

"God knows. Another of her crackpot whims I guess." He chuckled. "Couldn't miss out on a party though. What have you been up to lately?"

"Not a lot." I didn't mention our holiday, knowing that Frank wouldn't approve. Alice was the only one who got it – me and Oliver, I mean. I wanted encouragement, not sneers and snorts. Although, I had to admit, Alice wound me up most of the time, she didn't judge me. What's more, she was always greedy for every detail of our romance, and I needed a good listener. You see, I'd started to feel guilty about what I was doing to Oliver. After our day in Suffolk, I'd asked Alice's advice.

"This isn't going to work for him, is it?" I said.

"Don't think of it in conventional terms. You and Oliver have something special – a pure, untainted love," Alice had said. "God knows I never found that in my time on the earthly plane. Who needs the rest of the world? Find quieter places to be together. Enjoy each other. Forget everyone else."

Well, you know how it is when someone tells you exactly what you want to hear. I lapped up the advice and since then, we'd done just that. We'd rented a cottage in a quiet part of Brittany. It had been bliss: leisurely breakfasts that I tasted by licking Oliver's fingers, long walks along the rugged coastline, and sunbathing on the beach. We even read books together on his Kindle. It was the sort of memory that I'd have taken to my dying day, if I wasn't already dead.

Dave, a road accident victim, who must have done some bad stuff in his life because he'd kept every cut, every bruise, said. "Hi Rowena, Frank. Where's the guest of honour?"

"Waiting until we're all here, to make a big entrance, no doubt," said Frank.

He was right. Several minutes later, Alice appeared, and stood on a bench so that everyone could see her.

"My dear friends," she began. "My months in this realm have been the perfect opportunity to complete the studies I embarked upon in life. But the time has come to leave you."

It was all so over-the-top dramatic and so typically Alice that I had to bite on the inside of my mouth – yes, I could do that – to stop myself from giggling. Frank coughed and I think I detected the word, "bullshit" masked in the sound. Alice climbed down and started hugging everyone in turn.

"Surely she can't pick and choose when she passes?" I whispered.

"I dunno." Frank said. "Some people get tired of waiting and their body kind of fades away. I reckon she knows her time's coming. She's been having more and more of those funny turns, you know. Trust her to turn it into a pantomime."

"Hush, it's your turn."

"Frank, it's been … interesting." Alice said.

"It has, lass." Frank shook her hand.

Alice turned to me, and kissed me on each cheek.

"Your story moved me more than any other," she said. "Treasure what you've been given. And not just Oliver. Look around you; these are all your friends."

I looked around and realised that Alice was right; I was more popular here than I'd ever been, even before the accident. The nights on the Heath had become my equivalent of a night in the pub.

Once she'd finished the long rounds of goodbyes, Alice

asked everyone to stand in a circle and placed herself in the centre of it. She crossed her hands across her chest and looked towards the clear night sky, which was illuminated by a full moon, of course. It was hard not to giggle. Trust Alice to orchestrate the timing for maximum drama. But nothing happened for a few minutes. Frank snorted. I nudged him – poor Alice. What if she'd got it wrong? It would be so embarrassing.

At that moment, Christine cried out and pointed. Alice's hands were fading. I smiled and waited for that happy glow. But it didn't happen. And then there was a cracking sound, like fireworks. I couldn't believe what I was seeing – Alice's body appeared to explode. People screamed. Fragments of her body flew everywhere and then disintegrated. No-one spoke for a while. Then a hum of shocked conversations filled the space where Alice had been. Some people were even crying.

"Jesus wept. It's at times like this I crave a drop of a single malt," Frank said.

"Such an awful way to go," I said. "Remember your theory, about suicides having broken souls?"

"Yeah, huh, looks like I got summat right for once."

"I wonder if that's what happened to me and Oliver? Maybe someone committed suicide in a past life and their soul split in two."

"If you want to take my advice, lassie, I'd forget trying to make sense of any of this. Accept the fact that none of us know exactly what's in store. But if there's one lesson you can take from tonight, it's that you can't cheat death."

Frank's eyes bored into mine, and his message was an uncomfortable one. But was I cheating death? How did I know when my end would come?

CHAPTER 14

14th April 2015

"Generally, by the time you are Real, most of your hair has been loved off, and your eyes drop out and you get loose in the joints and very shabby. But these things don't matter at all, because once you are Real you can't be ugly, except to people who don't understand."

Oliver looked up and I sighed with satisfaction. These were my happiest times, when no-one existed except the two of us and all those fictional characters.

"You're right," he said, smiling at the copy of *The Velveteen Rabbit*. "It's a beautiful story. I can't believe I never read it."

"It was my favourite book when I was a kid," I said. "That and *Charlotte's Web*. I still think children's books have more wisdom in them than adult ones."

"Yeah, me too. I love the way they compress complex ideas into simple words. But we said we'd go out, didn't we? What do you think? We could go to Xscape."

"You're right, we should make the most of the weekend. But I'm not sure the artificial slope will be the same after the real thing," I smiled. Skiing had been one activity that Oliver didn't feel self-conscious doing alone. We'd found a small resort in Colorado. Oliver had booked himself private tuition and I'd run alongside him in the snow.

"It was magical out there, wasn't it?" He grinned.

"Yeah." My fingers brushed his chin. "I like your stubble when it's a couple of days old; it's soft," I murmured, placing my cheek against his to feel the tickle of the short hairs against my skin.

I stood up and looked out of the window. "It's brightened up. Why don't we go to the Heath and try that kite?"

That was another of our new games – listing all the things we'd wanted to do as kids and trying them out. Kite flying was one of Oliver's so we'd found a gorgeous rainbow-coloured stunt kite online.

"Yeah, why not?"

Soon we were walking towards the Heath, my hand in his pocket. We'd developed a sort of sign language. It wasn't exactly as satisfying as being able to talk in public, but at least he could let me know how he was feeling. Not that we needed it. I knew the workings of his mind so well that I could read every thought, but there was something special about this secret contact. He'd also got pretty good at talking while barely moving his lips.

"I was wondering about us going to one of the summer music festivals," he said.

"Yeah why not," I said. "You'll only have to buy one ticket; I'm such a cheap date. Though you'll have to go a long way to beat Colorado."

"You said that after Christmas. I like the challenge."

He was good at coming up with ideas. Spending the festive season in a cottage in the Scottish Highlands had been a romantic idyll. I'd smelled the wood smoke on Oliver's sweater. I'd encouraged him to make mulled wine and I swear I got drunk from the alcohol fumes and spices on his breath.

We were in luck; at the top of Parliament Hill, the sky was dotted with bright shapes bobbing in the breeze. And quite a few of the kite-fliers were on their own, freeing Oliver of any self-consciousness.

"Last time I did this I was about ten," I said. "My brother and his fiancée bought me a kite and taught me how to fly it. Hold the strings and release them slowly when I shout."

I shouted instructions but Oliver was a natural. Soon he was manoeuvring the kite like he'd been doing it all his life, not even aware of the people who were watching him admiringly. His pleasure was infectious, making me all the more startled when I heard a voice calling my name. I turned and saw Frank, watching from a bench.

"Oh my God, that's Frank," I said to Oliver. "I'd better go say hello. Can you manage without me for a few minutes."

"Yeah, it's child's play." He grinned.

I strolled over to Frank, stung by a pang of guilt. I hadn't been here for ages – I'd realised that using the night for rest helped me maximise my time with Oliver. But there'd been another reason. None of my other ghost friends listened to stories of Oliver with the enthusiasm that Alice had. In fact, I'd seen a few of them talking and nodding in my direction, then shutting up as soon as I came up to them. My popularity had definitely slipped. Even Frank had a new collection of snorts he saved for the mention of Oliver's name.

"So that's what you've been up to," said Frank. "I wondered what'd happened to you. Thought you must have passed over. It's been what, nearly six weeks since I saw you last? Everyone's been asking about you."

"Yeah, I guess it must be. Sorry, I keep meaning to come and say hi. What are you doing out in the day?"

"Been a bit restless lately. Jean's not been too well. Coughing something wicked."

"Oh, I'm sorry to hear that."

"Saw you walking with the laddie. Still having yourself a wee pretend romance are you? That knocks Alice's theory on the head. You don't vanish into a puff of smoke if he kisses you?"

"I don't know. We haven't risked kissing, just in case."

"Bloody hell, that's a shitty deal for the lad." Frank tutted and shook his head.

"It's not ideal, but it works," I said defensively. "We're in love, and it's … wonderful. I never came close to being as happy as this when I was alive."

"Aw come on, love, who are you trying to kid? I'm glad you've had yourself a bit of fun, but you can't ruin the poor lad's life like that."

"He's happy too. He tells me all the time."

"You're kidding yourself, if that's what you think. For him, it's only one step up from having an imaginary friend. He's a student, for God's sake. He should be taking drugs, going on protest marches and whatever else they do these days."

"We smoked a joint together last week. I inhaled it from his mouth."

Frank rolled his eyes. "And what about the other side of it?

He's a man. A red-blooded young man in his prime, and he has needs, if you get my meaning."

"He hasn't complained," I muttered.

"Take it from me, it won't be enough for him. Men can't exist on flowery words and holding hands. You're denying him a chance to live life to the full."

"We're doing plenty of other things. We've made a list of everything we ever wanted to do and –"

"Aye aye, look at that."

I followed Frank's stare and saw a girl around my age watching Oliver. Unsurprising, I guess. He looked wonderful in his new Levis and a white shirt. Hang on, she wasn't just watching, but walking right up to him! I'd better find out what was going on.

"You're really good with that kite," the simpering mare said. Hands off, he's mine, I wanted to scream, "I saw you launching it. How did you get it to stay in the air like that?"

Oliver glanced over his shoulder at me.

"Go on, talk to her. I can't hear from here," I lied.

"Er, I'm n-n-not sure. Wind just b-b-blowing in the right direction, I think."

Funny, I'd completely forgotten about his stammer. He was so fluent when he was with me that it was hard to believe that this awkward boy, who didn't know where to look, was the same person. Ha, that should put her off.

"I'm Judy," the girl said. She was small and pretty in a cute, wholesome sort of way. Even her clothes were cute – a short green patterned dress covered with owls, thick black tights and black suede boots. I wasn't exactly built like a carthorse but I felt huge in comparison. I hated her.

"H-hi, I'm Oliver."

"Can I have a go?"

Oliver handed Judy the line then glanced at me with an apologetic shrug. Judy flew the kite for about thirty seconds, before it crashed into the ground.

"I'm hopeless." Judy gave a self-deprecating laugh. You know the type. Pretending to be modest but fishing for compliments. Pathetic.

"N-no, that was p-p-pretty good for a beginner," Oliver said.

"Do you fancy a coffee?" she said.

It was one of those breath-holding, jaw-tightening moment where my fake body behaved exactly like a real one.

"N-no thanks. I'm with … I m-mean, I'm m-meeting s-s-someone."

Judy's head dipped. "Oh, OK, I'll be seeing you." She walked away.

Frank joined me.

"See what I mean?" he said. "Perfectly nice lass; he might have found himself a proper girlfriend there if you hadn't got in the way. Poor lad can't have a normal life as long as you're around."

He raised his hand in farewell and walked away.

"But he's got a proper girlfriend!" I said and started crying.

Oliver had been gathering in the strings and now turned to me.

"What did you say? Hey, what's up?" he mouthed.

"Nothing. Just felt a bit faint. Think I'll sit over there for a minute."

I sat on the bench, digesting what Frank had said. He was right. Of course he was. I'd been so wrapped up in my happy little bubble that I hadn't thought about the future. I trudged back towards Oliver. My voice, when it came out, didn't sound like my own.

"She was cute, wasn't she? Did you like her? Did you want to ask her out?"

"No, course not," he said between immobile lips "Why would I look at anyone else when I've got you?" Then his face split into a grin. "Oh my God, that's it. You're jealous!" he said out loud, then clamped his hand to his mouth, looked around and blew his breath out in relief that no-one seemed to have noticed.

"But you haven't got me, have you? I'm not flesh and blood. She is." Why couldn't I control my voice? Why did it sound so shrill?

"Come on, let's get you home," he said, and reached for my hand.

We spent the afternoon in our favourite way, watching a film, Oliver's head in my lap; me stroking his hair. But Frank's words hammered in my head. When we played our sensory games, I felt it, all right. That longing, kind of like an itch I couldn't scratch. For Oliver, it must be a million times worse. Was I being selfish? Of course I was.

"Oliver, isn't this relationship too frustrating for you? Physically, I mean."

The flush in his cheeks gave her me the answer before he even opened his mouth. "Well, yeah. Sometimes. I've even wondered if we could ... you know ... do more stuff without kissing." He swallowed. "But it's not worth the risk of losing you."

"Maybe we should do it all anyway. Maybe it's time for me to pass over. You shouldn't be living like this strange half-life." I stopped, and then forced out the words I didn't want to say. "It's been over a year now, and it's been ... better than anything I could ever have imagined, but we can't go on like this forever. You're halfway thorough your degree, and how much student life have you actually experienced? You should be getting drunk in bars, and going out with living girls like that one in the park."

He sat up.

"So that's what it's all about. You've been in a funny mood ever since we've got back. Rowena, it's you I love. We're soul mates. You know that. I don't know why it's got to be this way, but I'd rather share this half-life with you than a so-called normal life with anyone else. I love you, not just for who you are, but for the way I am when I'm with you. Before you, I was nothing."

"That's because you didn't make the effort. You should put yourself out there more. You've got so much to offer. You just need to believe it."

"But with you, I don't need to make an effort. With you, I'm not shy. With you I don't stammer. With you I feel I can conquer the whole world." His voice was so convincing, so thrillingly passionate, that I almost crumbled, but Frank's words reverberated in my ears. You're holding him back, holding him back, holding him back ...

"But you're not going to want to be with me forever, are you? This has to end at some stage. You're going to want to marry, have kids, all that stuff. Maybe we shouldn't prolong the agony."

"I dunno. Maybe I don't need all that. Maybe I'll just grow old with you." He chuckled. "Hey, I get the good deal in all this. I don't have to watch you getting old and wrinkled. It's every guy's dream, isn't it, always having a gorgeous young woman on their arm. Not so good for you, though, having to live with me when I'm old and drooling."

"A gorgeous young woman isn't much of a trophy if she's invisible. Anyway, you're already older than me." I smiled, but it faded. That's how it would be, wouldn't it? We'd get tired of having only each other's company in time; eventually we'd have said everything there was to say to each other. Oliver would end up old and lonely, having never done anything with his life, and he'd resent me. Maybe he'd stop loving me and we'd split up, then I'd carry on being a ghost even after he'd gone, and I'd have to wait for him in the next incarnation.

"Oliver, sweetheart, think about it logically. This isn't fair on you. I have to set you free."

I lunged towards him before I had time to talk myself out of it, and pressed my lips to his. But his lips were closed and rigid, resisting me. Then he shoved my away. I put my fingers to my lips, hurt and humiliated.

"It didn't work." There was a quiver in my voice.

"Course it didn't. I didn't kiss you back. You see, Rowena, you can only go when I choose." His voice had a sinister edge; his smile was satisfied, smug even.

"What if I begged you? What if I'm sick and tired of all this? I hate not being able to go out with you to bars and restaurants and clubs and all the things normal couples can do. What if I want to know what's on the other side?"

"Look me in the eye and tell me you don't want this any more." He softened his voice, hands cupping my face.

And of course I couldn't.

CHAPTER 15

23rd April 2015

"You were right; of course you were," I said to Frank. "I've known it all along. I just didn't want to face up to the truth, I guess."

"Yeah, well, that's understandable," he replied. We were sitting on a bench on Hampstead Heath, ignoring rain that bounced from the path in front of us.

"But if he won't release me, what can I do?"

"Help him, maybe. Boost his confidence. You've got us to talk to, but what's he got apart from you? Poor kid's frightened of real life."

"I listened to him on the phone last week when he didn't realise I was around. I couldn't believe how inarticulate he was without me." I put my fists to my eyes in an attempt to block the thought. "But when we're together, we complete each other."

He wagged his finger. "Stop all that romantic guff. What if you accidentally passed? It happens, you know. How would he cope then?"

"But … oh I know this is selfish, but I don't want to leave him. I mean … what if Alice was wrong, and we don't meet up in a different life? I'm still not sure I entirely believe in reincarnation. The nuns at school would have said we'd all be reunited with our loved ones in heaven. But does heaven exist? Would I ever see him again? To be honest, I'm terrified of passing over."

Frank scratched his head. "I don't know what to say to you, love. Far as I know, no-one's ever come back from the other side to give us the answers. But you saw how happy that young lass, Jasmine looked, before she went. It has to be a good place."

"Yeah, I felt that when I watched Marjorie pass too. Oh, it's not just that ... I can't stand to think of Oliver moving on and finding someone else. Maybe I've been caught up in a silly Mills and Boon delusion? Maybe I'm not his soul mate. Maybe soul mates don't even exist?"

"I don't reckon they do. Well, think about it. If there was just one man for every woman, what's the chances of finding them? I reckon that in any lifetime you'll come across ten or so people you could settle down with, and you've just got to hope you pick one of the right ten. But have you even thought that he might find someone else anyway? That young lass on the Heath took a fancy to him." His voice softened. "You think I'm not scared? And every other ghost who leaves someone behind? Jean was still in her forties when I kicked the bucket, a cracking looking woman. I always wondered if she'd find someone else. Used to wander round here, not being able to rest for worrying about it. They say people who've had a good husband or wife are way more likely to find another one. At least if you release him and afterwards he finds himself a lass, you won't be around to see it."

"I can't bear to even think about it." I stared at the grass.

"Hey, come on, love. This is all getting a bit gloomy, isn't it? I reckon that if the two of you are twin souls or whatever, you'll find each other again. You know what I made of Alice's half-baked theories, but even I can see that the fact that you're so real to each other – that's got to mean summat."

"Anyway, how's Jean?"

"Better, but I reckon her time's coming. I hope so. Truth is, I've had enough of all this. I'm tired."

"It does get tiring, doesn't it? I never noticed before." I'd been more present in the last year than in nineteen years of being with Marjorie. "I used be able to disappear almost at will. But now I'm with Oliver, I'm with him for all the time he's at home. And sometimes when he's at college, I end up alone in the house. He leaves the TV on for me, or an audiobook, but it can get pretty boring."

"You know as well as I do, you'll never keep this up for sixty-odd years. You need to prepare him."

He was right. But I needed help. By now it was obvious that the funny, confident guy I was in love with presented a completely different image to the rest of the world. If I was going to help him, I needed to get to know that other person, the awkward, stammering one. But how could I see that side of him? I needed to recruit another ghost, but Frank was my closest friend. I opened my mouth to ask him and then closed it again. It wasn't fair, not when Jean might need him. Maybe he wouldn't be around much longer. The thought was a depressing one. And then I remembered that I had another friend.

"Frank, when ghosts are asleep, is it dangerous to wake them up?"

"Not dangerous as such, just not very good manners, you might say. Remember when you woke me up, that first time? Can't say I was too chuffed about it. But it didn't do me no harm, did it? Why, who you gonna wake?"

"My friend, Kirsty. Remember me telling you? The one who died a year after me. She sleeps in Finchley Road Cemetery."

"And she's never woken in all that time?"

"I don't know. I've only been to see her a few times but she's always been asleep when I've been there."

"Take it easy on her, then. She might be a bit groggy when she wakes, or she might not even wake at all. And come and see me tonight and tell me all about it."

I skipped all the way to the cemetery. I'd wondered about doing it, before, but this last year I'd been so wrapped up in Oliver that I'd hardly thought of Kirsty. What sort of a friend was I?

The rain had eased to a drizzle by the time I made it to Kirsty's grave and there she was, curled up, looking exactly as she had last time I saw her.

"Kirsty." I didn't raise my voice at first and gave her a light shake of the shoulder.

Nothing.

"Kirsty, it's me!" A rougher shake.

And then she moved! She shuffled about a bit at first, then stretched and rubbed her eyes.

"Cyclops?" She squinted and sat up. Her eyes darted

everywhere. "Where are we? What's going on?" Her voice was slurry, a little like she was drunk, even though I know she never touched anything stronger than cider when she was alive. And she seemed terrified. Maybe this had been a mistake.

I linked my arm through hers, the way we used to.

"You know you're …"

"Dead," she interrupted. "Yeah, so why do I feel so sleepy?"

"I can explain it all. But what do you remember since you died?"

"I remember sort of rising over my body and just hanging around, watching them all crying. And I thought I saw you, but you disappeared. Then, the next thing I knew, five whole years had passed. I was in a pokey bedroom with my little brother who wasn't so little any more. After a while I worked out that he'd just started college, so I guess he was around eighteen. He seemed kind of lost, and I tried talking to him, but he didn't hear me. And then … I dunno, I remember the room spinning, then nothing. Have I skipped another few years or is this heaven? Hey, your face!"

That was the point when I realised what a selfish mistake I'd made. All I'd thought about was the need to be with Kirsty, not what this might do to her.

"No, we're still on earth. It's 2015."

"Shit, no. What, so it's eighteen years since I died? What am I – some sort of ghost?"

"Uh … yeah." It took me a long time to explain it all to Kirsty, but by the time I'd finished, she'd calmed down.

"So all this time, I've been sleeping? Hell, why didn't you wake me sooner? We could have had all sorts of fun."

"I wasn't sure if I could, or should. I guess there's a reason you're sleeping."

"So what's 2015 like? Is it like *Back to the Future* – hoverboards and all that?"

"Nowhere near as good as that." I grinned. "God, I've missed you."

"Why aren't I cold?" She looked at her oversized T shirt and grinned. And have I got any knickers on?" She reached to check. "Oh yeah. Thank God for that."

"I wouldn't worry. No-one except me and other ghosts can see you," I said.

"Can I see my folks? And my brother – he was 13 in '96 so that means … he'll be 32 now! Oh my God! He could be married with kids and all sorts!"

Ugh, I'd been stupid, hadn't I? I should have checked up on all sorts before I woke Kirsty up. What if her folks had moved out of London? Died, even? No, they weren't that old – I guess they'd be in their sixties by now.

"Um, I don't know if your folks are still in their old house, but we could see." Kirsty soon mastered the knack of running quickly and it only took us five minutes to reach her parents' house. Then I had to teach her the walking-through-doors trick.

"This is so cool!" She gasped, looked around, and her smile faded.

As soon as we stood in the hallway I could tell her folks had moved. They were pretty young and cool as parents go, but no way would they have an arty black and white nude on the wall.

"Fuck! How will I ever find them?"

"There's ways. These days everyone has the internet and you can find everything just by touching a screen. Oliver could find them for us.

"Oliver?"

"Yeah. He's my boyfriend." I'd already given Kirsty so much to get her head around, I hadn't told her anything about myself.

"How the hell can you have a boyfriend?"

"Well, it's another long story …" which I told her in every detail, ending with "So I was feeling like I needed a friend, and I wasn't sure if it was right to disturb you, but knowing you were there –"

"I just can't believe I've missed so much. So let's go see your Oliver."

"He'll be in college today."

"Let's give him a surprise, then."

"Oh, I couldn't do that. It's not fair on him, you see. Imagine how it looks to the other guys, him smiling and talking to a ghost that they can't see."

"When does he get home?"

"Around six, usually. Tell you what, why don't you and I can have a look round London and I can show you what's changed."

"Excellent!"

Six hours later, we were still giggling and gossiping. I'd forgotten how much fun it used to be, hanging round with Kirsty. We'd spent the day in Top Shop, looking at all the new fashions, as well as the tourist attractions she'd never seen.

"Size 6. They didn't even have that when I got so skinny, Everything hung on me," she said.

"Everyone's skinny these days," I told her. "And chart music's crap. I preferred things back in the nineties."

"But that London Eye's the best thing ever!" Kirsty said.

"Me and Oliver love it."

"Get you. It's me and Oliver this, me and Oliver that. Don't the two of you ever disagree on anything?"

"No. Funnily enough, we hardly do."

"Isn't that a bit boring?"

"It sounds like it should be, but it isn't. Ah, here he is."

"Oh my God! That's him. He's lush! You lucky cow."

"Hi sweetheart." I jumped up to hug him.

"Hiya gorgeous. What're you laughing at?"

"You remember me telling you about my friend Kirsty? She's here!"

"What, right here?" He frowned.

"Hey, right here." Kirsty stood in front of him and grabbed his crotch. I dissolved into fifty fits of laughing. But I saw the discomfort flicker across Oliver's face. He hated being made fun of. Suddenly, I wished Kirsty wasn't here.

"Hi, Kirsty, wherever you are," said Oliver, with the false smile I'd come to recognise. "So what have you two been up to?"

I told him about our day, but I wanted Kirsty to leave us, and somehow, I must have transmitted this thought to her because she clutched her head and said, "Shit, Ro, I've gone all dizzy."

"It's OK, I'll find you again tomorrow. See you later."

And Kirsty disappeared.

"What the hell's going on?" Oliver said, his mouth set tight.

"I decided to see if I could wake Kirsty. We had the best day together."

"Where's this come from?" He frowned. "You haven't mentioned her for ages. And you never do anything without talking about it with me first."

"I know, I was feeling kind of lonely, that's all. Thought it'd be fun to have someone to hang out with during the day. But I didn't think it through. Her family have moved away and she wants to know what's happened to them. Can we look them up on the internet?"

"We can try, depends on how unusual their names are."

"Her surname's Lofthouse. Her mum's called Sue and her dad's called Paul."

"Seriously? We're talking needles and haystacks. Look." He Googled Paul Lofthouse and I saw his point.

"Maybe her brother's a better bet. He's called Jason and he was a talented artist."

"Doesn't mean he became one." Oliver frowned and set to his searching again. Soon he looked up triumphantly. "I tried Jason Lofthouse, design and found this."

I looked at the website – a graphic design company with a Crouch End address. There was also a photo. Kirsty's little brother had been thirteen when I'd last seen him but it was easy to imagine that he'd have grown up to be this fashion victim with the same grey eyes as Kirsty.

I woke Kirsty the next day. She rubbed her eyes and took in the cemetery.

"So that's what happens, is it? I go back to sleeping here?"

"Yes. Some people are called somewhere else, like me. But people who died of natural causes before they reach eighteen seem to sleep most of the time."

"So how come you wake up on your own and I have to wait to see you? That's not fair."

"I guess … because Oliver needs me." That sounded tactless, didn't it? But I guess it must be true; no-one needed Kirsty to be around. I could see her eyes dip so I launched straight into the good news. "Anyway, guess what? I might have found your brother." I told her the details.

"Oh my God! Can we go see him?"

"Yes, we can get the tube to Highgate then a fifteen minute walk, which we can do in five minutes."

Soon we'd found the office, above a shop in Crouch End Broadway.

"Wow, look at these chairs. It's all so … futuristic!" I swear Kirsty's eyes were bulging. It was a cool place, all grey and purple, very designer-y. We were in a small reception area, empty until a gorgeous blond guy emerged from an adjoining room, and Kirsty launched herself at him, only to pass straight through him. He blinked, but there was no other reaction.

"Jase!" she squealed then turned to me, disappointed.

"He can't hear me," she muttered.

"That's normal," I said.

"So what's the point in seeing them if he can't see me?"

"Look at this!" I flung my arm around the room. "He's successful. Surely it's worth something to know that."

"Yeah, I guess so." Kirsty managed a smile. "But I still want to know what happened to Mum and Dad."

"So we follow Jason home. There'll be clues there. He'll visit them occasionally. If you're meant to see them, you will."

"Sounds like claptrap to me."

"Trust me. It just takes patience."

"Huh, haven't got much choice, have I?" Kirsty said. "I can't wake up without you. So what are we up to today?"

"Well, there's something I need you to do. I didn't explain it yesterday, but I want to help Oliver – I know he's not confident without me."

"Seemed confident enough yesterday. He looked pretty pissed off to find out that I was there, though. Don't think he likes sharing you."

"What do you mean?" I said, even though I knew exactly what she meant.

"Well, to be honest, I think your so-called relationship's a bit weird. I mean, yeah, it looks like he's nuts about you, but it seemed like he kind of owned you at the same time, and that can't be good."

"Well, it's not exactly conventional, is it? His friends can't see me and he can't see my friends."

Kirsty shook her head. "So what is it you want me to do?"

"I want to make sure that … if anything happens to me, that he'll be all right without me. But I don't know just how bad he is. I need you to stalk him. Follow him for a whole day, watch all of his interactions with other people. And in return, I'll try and find out where your Mum and Dad are."

"Cool, an invisible stalker! You've got yourself a deal. So where am I going?"

I directed Kirsty to Oliver's college building. I'd travelled in with him before, but never inside the building. "I know he has a lecture at ten; check out all the lecture theatres."

While Kirsty took off to be a spectator in Oliver's day, I went back to Jason's office. I listened to every conversation, but got no clues about his parents, so followed him home, an achingly trendy flat about five minutes walk from his office. I liked to think that I'd been broad-minded, but I was surprised to see Jason kissing a man, open-mouthed, who appeared to live with him and share his bed. Feeling like I was intruding too much, I scanned the flat, and found a collage of photos. Oh wow, there was Kirsty, looking exactly as she still did, but a photo that must be nearly twenty years old. And another photo – I let out my breath – of their parents, older and greyer than I remembered. But what was Kirsty doing in the photo? I shook myself – was my mind playing tricks on me? Then I realised that the girl in the picture wasn't Kirsty, just someone who looked a lot like her. But Kirsty's mum was under forty when Kirsty died, young enough to have another baby. Oh no. Should I tell her?

Luckily, Kirsty was so entertained by the fact of having a gay brother, that I didn't mention the possibility of her having a sister.

"Ha, I wonder what Dad made of it?" she giggled. "I'm not surprised at all. So what does his boyfriend look like?"

"Nice, in an over-trendy sort of way," I said. "Hair cropped at the back and sides, with a zigzag line shaved through it."

"Cool, can we go see them?"

"Well not now, Oliver will be back soon. So, did you find him?"

"Yeah, but you won't like it," she said. "Ro, you're sure he's your soul mate?"

"Yeah, why?" Icy dread shot through me. What had she seen?

"At the college, it was like seeing a different person. It took me ages to hear his stammer because he hardly ever speaks, but when he does, it's bad. He hangs round with a couple of guys but they're the biggest geeks in what doesn't look like the coolest class in the first place. Seriously, he's a good-looking guy, but I don't know what you see in him. He's the sort of guy we'd have called a loser."

It was what I'd been expecting, but to have her say it so bluntly came as a shock.

"So I can't set him free yet," I muttered.

"Hang on, how exactly are you going to set him free?"

"By kissing him, of course."

"You really think that's gonna work?"

"It's all I've got."

"Well … I think you've got a bit of work to do if he's gonna cope on his own."

And between us, Kirsty and I devised a plan. We were going to teach Oliver how to live.

CHAPTER 16

30th April 2015

"You're miles away," said Oliver, his eyes darkened with suspicion. "That usually means you're plotting something."

"Not really. Just daydreaming." I grinned. The more I thought about my plan, the more I realised that I had a reason to stick around. Building up Oliver to be able to face the world on his own wasn't going to happen overnight. "But I've been thinking. We need to get you out more. You haven't been out with your college mates for ages."

Oliver's mouth twisted into a scowl. "What is it? You've got your new ghost friend to play with, so you want me out of the way first?" His voice was hard, cruel even, not like him at all.

"It's not that. In fact, I didn't wake Kirsty today. She asked me if she could sleep for a few days, said she was tired. It's just ... this isn't enough for you. No matter how much we kid ourselves, it makes life easier if you're confident with people, doesn't it? And you can't hide in here with me all the time; next year you'll have to find a job. You need to be better prepared for the real world."

"I'll work in IT. You don't exactly have to be dynamic." He shrugged. "But I guess you've got a point ..."

"And it'd help me too. I think I need more time to rest. Kirsty's not the only one who's tired. When you went on that residential course last month, I disappeared for three whole days, and afterwards, I felt like I'd had a good sleep."

Oliver's eyes became soft. "You never told me. I had no idea you got tired."

"It's something I've only noticed lately. I think it's because I don't skip time any more, the way I did with your nan." I squeezed his hand. "I just thought it might be good for both of us. Don't the guys from college ever go out for a drink?"

"Some of them do, every Friday, but not the ones I hang round with. I've been a couple of times, but you know I'm not all that good in groups. They never ask me, these days."

"Maybe you should ask them."

"I dunno …"

"Would it help if I went with you at first?"

He grinned. "It might. Could be a bit distracting, but I guess we could give it a go. You won't play any tricks or make me laugh, will you?"

"You'll never know until we try. If nothing else, it'll give us something new to talk about."

I knew I'd won my first victory.

And so, on Friday, I found myself at Imperial College. It certainly wasn't how I imagined student life – everyone was hunched over a desk, working. So many computers in one place! I caught sight of Oliver's red head bent over a screen from across the room, and felt that giddy rush I still had whenever I saw him for the first time in the day. I rushed to his side and brushed his hair.

"Hi sweetheart," I said. "There's a couple of guys over there putting their coats on. Are they the ones?"

He moved his head so slightly that only I noticed. He shut down the computer, said goodbye to a guy next to him who pushed a strand of greasy hair from his eyes – I guess he was one of the major geeks Kirsty had mentioned – and then looked towards the other guys. To be fair, they looked okay – just normal guys: jeans, T shirts with names of bands on them, fleece jackets, canvas shoes. You might not pick them out in a police line-up, but they looked like the sort of people you wouldn't mind having a drink with. Oh no, Oliver was looking at them like they were the coolest, most unapproachable guys on the planet. How had I never seen this side of him?

"Do you need me to prompt you?" I said.

A tiny shake of the head.

"OK, just stride over to them like you've been mates for years," I said.

He approached the group, and said with only a slight wobble, "Y-you off for a drink?" His voice was a little quiet.

I'd talk to him about that, later.

"Yeah, fancy joining us?" one said with a hint of a frown.

"Yeah …" Oliver said and seemed to get stuck for what to say next.

"I could do with a pint." I prompted.

"I could do with a pint," Oliver said.

"Blimey, we're honoured," a second student said.

I saw Oliver's face fall, but I hadn't done all that people watching for nothing.

"I know he sounded sarcastic, but he's genuinely pleased you're joining them," I said.

Oliver turned as if about to reply but I shook my head and nodded to the door. Together with four other students, they left the building, making small talk, and headed for a student bar. I couldn't help getting a bit excited, a chance to witness student social life, something I'd once dreamed of. At first I didn't feel I was missing much. The bar was all light wood and looked more like a school canteen than a pub but on the walls were posters advertising society meetings, gigs, charity parachute jumps, all sorts. Oliver should be grabbing these opportunities by the balls, making the most of all the time he had, free of responsibility. Once the daily grind of a nine to five kicked in, when would he get the chance again?

I shook myself out of my thoughts and focussed on the present. Oliver hadn't said a lot so far, but he was doing OK.

"Offer to buy the drinks now, before someone else does," I said, seeing that Oliver was the last to enter. "And raise your voice a little."

"I'll get these, lads. What are you having?" Oliver said.

"Cheers, mate. Pint of lager."

The others gave their orders and found a table. I stood next to Oliver at the bar.

"This is the bit I hate, getting served," he muttered.

"With your height and looks, it should be easy. It seems to me that the best way to get attention in one of these places is to have your arm held upwards with money in your hand," I said.

Oliver did as I said and was soon served. Another of his unfounded and irrational beliefs broken. He took a tray full of drinks to the table and joined the others. I crouched by the side of him and tried not to giggle when I heard the topic of conversation.

"Did you see that skirt Lisa was wearing, or should I say, half a skirt?" said the taller of the guys.

"Yeah, she's well fit," I prompted and then laughed. "God, I can't believe I'm saying this."

Oliver raised his eyebrow, the corners of his mouth turning upwards.

"Yeah, she's well fit," he repeated.

"You may be in with a shout there, Ollie. That is, I guess you're not seeing anyone?"

"No, I live with a ghost!" I said and then stopped myself. What if he repeated it?

"Well, sort of," Oliver said. "I mean, there is someone, but it's not serious."

I swatted his ear. "Ooh, I'm wounded."

"Yeah? What's she like?" The other guys were leaning towards him now, obviously taking an interest.

"Absolutely stunning." I stood up and assumed a model pose.

"She's gorgeous," Oliver said. "But drives me up the wall half the time. Think it might be time to call it a day."

For a nanosecond I thought he was being serious. But when I placed my hand on his thigh, he gave it a stroke. He was enjoying this as much as I was! By the time the group broke up, an hour later, we were both giggling.

"That was brilliant!" I said. "You were doing so well towards the end."

"Only because you keep making me laugh," Oliver muttered. "But it was fun. I admit. Did they say anything about me when I went to the toilet?"

"The tall one – Richard? – said that your stammer had improved; he thought that maybe you'd had speech therapy. And the Asian guy said that you were a good laugh and wondered why you didn't come out more often."

"Ugh, I hate the stammer. I know that some people avoid me because they just find it embarrassing."

"Then they're not the sort you should be hanging out with. These guys are. They seem like decent people and they like you."

He smiled, but it wasn't a relaxed smile. I still had plenty of work to do.

The tube journey home was vile. People crammed themselves into the space I occupied, a sensation I'd never become comfortable with. But I'd got carried away with my success, and on the walk along Muswell Hill Broadway I noticed a poster on a hall window that read: 'Speed dating, 16th May'.

"You should totally do that!" I said.

"What would I want to do that for?" he asked. "I've got a stunning girlfriend."

"Because it would be good practice. I mean, it wouldn't matter what you said, you'd never have to see these girls again. It's the perfect way to experiment with the sort of small talk the rest of the world takes for granted. Besides, I want to see how it works. It could be a giggle."

"No, no, and no way," he said.

But two things I'd learned in twenty years were patience and persistence. Eventually Oliver agreed to go. But before that, I had a breakthrough on the Kirsty front.

"Ro, how long since I saw you last?" Kirsty had the slightly slurred voice that she always had when woken.

"Ten days," I said. "But I had to wake you today because I saw something on Jason's computer calendar. He's going to your Mum and Dad's tonight." I still hadn't plucked up the courage to tell her about her new sister.

"What's the date?"

"May 8th."

"Ah, it's Mum's birthday tomorrow. Maybe that's why."

"So I'll put you in his car when he leaves work. Then just go with it, you'll get pulled back here when you've had enough."

"But you've got to come with me," she insisted.

"I can't. It's Friday night. Me and Oliver always watch a film on Fridays."

"Oh God, will you listen to yourself? How old are you – nineteen or ninety? Besides, if I slip back too early, I'll need you to wake me up again."

She won, of course, much to Oliver's annoyance. That evening found me standing on the street with Kirsty, watching Jason put a small case and a printed bag into the boot of their red car, which, like them, looked sleek and swish. I couldn't tell what type, except that the badge had four overlapping circles and the letter TT.

"How much do you need?" Tim said to Jason, with a roll of the eyes. "We're only staying for two nights."

"Staying!" Kirsty said to me with a grin.

We leapt into the back, which appeared to have been designed to seat two pygmies.

"Shit, do ghosts get cramp?" Kirsty said. "How long will we have to be hunched up like this?"

"Ah, we don't need to," I said. "If you concentrate hard enough, you can spread yourself out. I pressed my knees against the back of the driver's seat and, sure enough, they sank into the leather upholstery. Kirsty soon mastered it. Don't ask me how it worked – I don't make the rules. Logically we should have sunk through the seats, shouldn't we? Ah well, there had to be some benefits to being a ghost.

After about forty minutes, the car turned off the motorway.

"So they moved out of London?" Kirsty sat up, looking at the road signs. "Where's this? Buckinghamshire?"

"I think so."

Soon the car pulled into the driveway of a semi-detached house. A typical suburban-looking building with a bay window and roses in the front garden, set in a quiet street full of similar-looking houses. The sort of place you'd probably want to live when you retired.

"Mmm, nice … Oh my God, MUM!" Kirsty bolted out of the car to where a woman was standing at the open door. She was ageing well – she was still slim enough to wear jeans and not look ridiculous. Pretty cool for a woman who was pushing sixty. In fact, Kirsty was just telling her how good she looked. But of course her mum couldn't see her. And then the girl from the photo came out. She looked a little older now and was wearing a purple cotton dress together with black leggings and purple Doc Martens. He hair was so straight it looked like it had been ironed, and was half dark, half blonde. I couldn't even look at Kirsty.

"Jase!" the girl yelled.

And Jason ran up to her, lifted her up and swung her around.

"Look at you! Proper student!" he said and gazed at her with obvious affection.

"Who the fuck's she?" Kirsty was practically screaming.

"Calm down," I said. "If you get too worked up, you might send yourself back. I didn't want to tell you, but I've seen a photo of her in Jason's flat. Look, there's your Dad."

Kirsty's dad had now joined the group but Kirsty had hardly noticed; she couldn't take her eyes off this replacement version of herself. Maybe this was why Kirsty was sleeping. Maybe she wasn't meant to find this out. Had I screwed up big time by waking her?

We went into the house and while the family exchanged gossip – the new sister was called Poppy and was back from her first term at Birmingham University – Kirsty and I explored the house, looking for photos.

"Look, there's still one of you," I said. "They haven't forgotten you."

"But look of all these of her. That's how I remember Mum, and there's a baby in her arms. Huh, she didn't wait long to replace me, did she?"

"Maybe that was the best way for her to deal with her grief?" I was way out of my depth here; in truth I was just as shocked as Kirsty at how soon afterwards Poppy had been born.

"I've had enough of this. Don't wake me again. I don't want to know about their happy families any more."

Kirsty stumbled out of the house, but had hardly reached the end of the driveway when her body disappeared. And then I felt myself going dizzy and soon I'd gone too.

※ ※ ※

"You get yourself into more messes than anyone I ever met. But you can fix this," Frank said. It was almost a week before I'd rematerialised, a day before Oliver's speed dating evening. Oliver thought I'd be best to leave Kirsty alone from now on. It was one of the few times I'd disagreed with him.

"I don't think I can fix it, not Kirsty, anyhow. God, you were right about everything. I've made a young guy completely dependent on me. I've messed up my best friend's eternal rest. And I'm so bloody tired. I'm terrified I'm going to fade away before I have time to get Oliver anywhere near ready to survive the big bad world."

"You'll do it, love. And don't give up on Kirsty. Maybe you need to spy on her family a bit more. There's bound to be some time when they commemorate her death. Her anniversary, birthday perhaps. Bring her back for that, show her that they loved her."

"Frank, I hope one day I get as wise as you." I smiled. "That's it! She died in February – that's a long time to wait, but let me think her birthday's in June! But what if they don't mention it? Some families don't, you know."

"Then you wait until February. Don't worry. You've got a mission. You'll still be here, not like me." Jean was in and out of hospital these days.

"But I guess you're ready to go?" I asked, trying to lighten my tone, to hide how upset I felt. It was hard to imagine not having Frank to talk to.

"I am, lass. Come on now, give me that smile." I pasted on a grin. "You'll do it. Never saw a ghost with such a big heart as you."

***

The next day saw me in a pub, next to Oliver, mouths gaping.

"This is surreal," I said.

The normal arrangement of tables and chairs had shifted and a line of fifteen tables ran along the centre of the room.

"Not exactly romantic, is it?" he muttered. "Oh shit, look at my first 'date'. She has to be at least forty. Thought they were meant to be age 18 to 35."

"Likes the tanning salon as well, doesn't she? That skin would glow in the dark," I said. "Oh well, go for it. We'll laugh about it afterwards."

Oliver took his seat and I shuffled up behind him to listen.

"So how old are you, hon?" the woman said. Up close, I could see the wrinkles around her eyes and deep grooves around her mouth when she smiled.

"Twenty," Oliver said.

"Aw, you could be my toy boy. I'm thirty-three."

"Sure you are," I said.

Oliver let out a sound that was part splutter, part snort. I stepped back.

"Sorry, I'll keep it zipped," I promised. "Don't want to get you banned."

But intriguingly, Oliver threw himself into it. Each time he took on a different persona and experimented with different conversational openings, and mostly, they worked. I only laughed out loud once more, when a woman spent almost all the allotted time talking about her exes.

"And he complained about the fact that I didn't wax my legs for one whole day!" she said. "When it's never even occurred to him to wax his back! Oh no, our time's nearly up and you haven't told me anything about yourself. Any exes as vile as mine?"

"I finished with my last one because she talked too much," Oliver said, his expression deadpan. What I loved most was the way it went straight over the woman's head. And then he was saved by the bell.

"Thank God I'll never have to do anything like that," I said afterwards. "That one with glasses, Sheila, was the best, wasn't she?"

"You reckon? Desperate and needy, I thought. So how did I do?"

"You do best when you try the self-deprecating humour. Number three, Janice, didn't seem keen at first, but when you made that crack about being the only person to come out with a negative score average, she looked you in the eye for the first time. They all seemed interested when you talked about skiing; the enthusiasm showed in your eyes. Oh, and were you trying to be flirty with that bubbly girl – Bethany was it? It didn't quite work, but it was worth a try."

I carried on picking through Oliver's successes and failures and he considered my thoughts with the intense concentration of an earnest schoolboy in a maths class.

"We really are saddos aren't we?" he said. "I bet no-one else analyses it as much as we do."

"You'd be surprised. I eavesdropped on Sheila and Kate as we were leaving," – looks like they're friends – "and they were doing just the same as we are now."

"You haven't told me who ticked me," he said. "And don't

pretend you didn't look. I saw you looking over everyone's shoulder at the end of the sessions."

"You'll find out tomorrow; you had four matches." I grinned. "But you had five ticks. Sheila seemed well keen. And as for the ones who didn't, two were the ones you probably offended."

"Only five out of ten?" His shoulders slumped.

"That was great! Most people averaged three."

I carried on reassuring him until the dizziness struck.

"Hey, you OK?" he said.

"Yeah, but don't be surprised if I disappear in a minute. I'm not used to these late nights."

But it was another six days before I materialised.

In teaching Oliver how to live successfully, it appeared I was losing my own time.

CHAPTER 17

25th June 2015

I found myself on the sofa beside Oliver.

"What day is it?" I said.

"Wednesday, June 25th. You've been away since Sunday."

"Ah, sorry."

"It's OK. I can cope, you know." At first, he'd panicked if I had a couple of days away but this time he seemed calm. We were making incredible progress. I wasn't calm, though.

"Oh shit, I'd better stick around. Saturday's the big day."

I'd been popping in on Jason regularly – I couldn't remember the exact date of Kirsty's birthday – but had struck gold last week.

"We can't do next weekend, remember?" Jason had said to Tim

"Oh shit, yes, I almost forgot. Kirsty's birthday."

I hugged myself. So they did commemorate it!

"You'll be fine," Oliver said, pulling me out of my reverie. "You need a couple of relaxing evenings with me." He was right. The trips outside tended to exhaust me most. Being alone with him was heaven. "And one thing less for you to worry about. I've got something to do on Saturday."

"Ooh, what?" I said with a mixture of excitement and dread. Every step of progress that Oliver made came with a sting. One day he'd tell me he'd met a girl and although I knew it would be for the best, the thought terrified me.

"Ed at college has two tickets for Wimbledon and was meant to be taking his girlfriend, but they split up. He's asked me to go."

"Oh, you lucky thing," I said. "I went a few years ago – I've gatecrashed most big sporting events in London. Couldn't have any strawberries and cream though."

"Lucky I have some here, isn't it?"

And soon Oliver and I were playing our favourite games. One day we'd go too far, I was sure of it. But not yet, I had work to do.

***

"Kirsty, wake up!"

"Whassup … ugh, it's you. I told you I didn't want you to wake up again."

"I couldn't leave you like that, could I? So upset. Besides, today's a special day. Happy birthday!"

"How did you remember? Where've you been?"

"Never forgot my best mate's birthday. Anyway, make your mind up. You said you didn't want to see me again."

"Oh … I'm glad you woke me, I guess." She rubbed her eyes.

"Come on, shift yourself. We've off to Jason's."

"Jason's?"

Within minutes, we were inside Jason and Tim's flat. But – oh, no – there was a visitor I wasn't expecting. Poppy, today wearing a red-and-white stripy dress over her leggings. Then I heard what she was saying. Interesting.

"What the fuck's SHE doing here? You trying to rub my nose in it even more?" Kirsty growled.

"Shut up and listen." I dug her in the ribs.

" – point of me being here?" Poppy said.

"You know Mum and Dad like it to be a family day," Jason said.

"So they can remind me even more that I don't measure up to my perfect dead sister? Kirsty never got suspended from school. Kirsty wouldn't get dragged out of a pub at fifteen. Kirsty wouldn't be getting shit grades at uni."

"Come on, Pops, it's not as bad as all that," Jason said. "Of course our memories of Kirsty are mostly good; she didn't live long enough to seriously screw up her life. You've got to remember, she was sick for two years before she died. But she had her moments. She wasn't the saint Mum and Dad make her out to be."

"I'm being a bitch, aren't I?" Poppy muttered.

"Little bit, but I can see where you're coming from.

Sometimes I used to think they'd have preferred it if I'd died and not her."

"Glad it's not just me. It's just, like, sometimes it's hard, y'know? I feel left out when you all start talking about her."

"You'd have loved her, you know. She was a lot like you. She'd definitely have been out there, getting herself into trouble if she'd been able to go out more."

Kirsty was gazing at her sister with new eyes. She turned to me.

"I kinda like her," she muttered. "Y'know, I always wanted a sister."

At that moment, Kirsty's parents arrived, with bags full of albums. It looked as if this was a family ritual. We stood behind the sofa, watching page after page of photos of Kirsty, charting the progress of her short life. Then we came to one of the two of us. I'd forgotten how bad my face used to look.

"Who's this?" Poppy said.

"Rowena," Jason said and turned to Tim. "Kirsty's best friend. God, I loved her. Really bright, she was. She'd help me with my homework."

"Inseparable, those two were." Kirsty's mum said. "And such a tragedy; she died a year before Kirsty, an accident, defending her landlady against burglars. Kirsty never got over it; hardly went out after that and her health went downhill fast, like she'd lost the will to live. They found her a bone marrow donor, you know, but she never got strong enough for the transplant."

I squeezed Kirsty's hand. She'd never told me that.

"I'd like to think they were up there together, laughing and joking the way they used to," said Kirsty's dad.

"And drinking cider." Jason giggled.

They carried on reminiscing, the sentimental sort of day that gave me a warm, fuzzy sort of feeling, like being wrapped in a fleece blanket, and I could see that Kirsty was enjoying it too. Then we noticed Poppy slip out.

"She looks upset," said Kirsty. "Let's follow her."

We found her crying in the toilet and talking on her mobile.

"Cazza? Sorry, just had to talk to someone. It's Perfect Kirsty Day … oh, I know, I know. But how the hell am I going to tell them? … no, I puked a bit this morning, but OK otherwise."

"Shit, she's pregnant!" Kirsty said.

"Poor kid," I muttered.

We listened to the rest of the conversation and the gist of it seemed to be that Poppy wasn't sure whether to have an abortion but wanted to talk it through with her folks. Eventually she hung up and burst into a fresh flood of tears.

Kirsty crouched beside her.

"Hey, sis, it's gonna be OK," she said.

"Who said that?" she muttered.

"You can hear me?"

Poppy didn't appear to hear, the second time. But she stopped crying, as if Kirsty's presence had comforted her. She returned to the living room, leaving Kirsty open-mouthed.

"I don't get it. Either she sees and hears me or not, surely?"

"I don't know. Frank said that his wife sometimes heard him, other times not. But there's definitely a connection there."

"Do you think I could become a sort of guardian angel to her, the way you were to Marjorie and Oliver?"

"Hmm, maybe. Remember, I used to follow Oliver around but I'd always come back to Marjorie, as if I was waiting for him. Perhaps the time's right for you and Poppy; she certainly seems like she needs help right now."

"How do I do it?"

"Go home with her, this evening. At least that way, you'll find out where she lives. You might get pulled back to the cemetery, but if it's meant to be, you might find yourself with her another time."

"That'd be incredible. I'm kinda scared, though. I've got a feeling you're not going to be around for that much longer, and I'd like to come back from time to time."

I had that feeling too.

"Who knows, hon? But I'll come to the cemetery every Monday morning, how's that? I think you can handle the rest of today on your own, now, don't you?"

And in proof that I still had control over my life, or whatever you want to call it, I faded from the scene and found myself back on Oliver's sofa later that evening, just as he returned.

"How did you manage that? I thought you'd still be with Kirsty."

"She's fine on her own now. How was the tennis?"

"Brilliant!" And for the rest of the evening we hardly stopped talking, both bursting to tell the stories of our day, just a normal couple interacting with the world, not hiding from it.

On Monday morning, Kirsty looked so happy in her sleep, I hardly wanted to wake her. But I had to know.

"So?" I said.

"She saw me!" Kirsty said. "Mum and Dad stayed until mid-afternoon, but she didn't tell them. When Jase got back in from seeing off Mum and Dad, I shouted, 'Tell him, Pops.' And she said, 'Who *is* that?' So I told her. And she said 'Kirsty?' She actually said my name! Jase gave her the third degree about what she thought she'd heard and persuaded her that it was in her mind. But she told him about the baby. And he persuaded her that she has to get an abortion – he found a clinic online and he's booked her in on Thursday – but I'm not sure that's what she wants. Anyway, I followed her home – she lives in Hatfield and she's just finishing her first year at Hertfordshire University – and when it was just me and her alone in her flat, I said, 'You don't have to do this.' And just for a minute, she looked right at me and said, 'Oh my God, it really is you!' Her words were getting faster and faster until they were running into each other."

"Whoa, slow down," I said. "How do you know what she wants?"

"It's ... I dunno, I can't explain it. It's like I could read her mind."

"So she's your special person," I said. "What happened after that?"

"I kind of went dizzy but when I woke up, I was still in her flat! She didn't see me or hear me this time, but it was so nice to just watch her, living the sort of life I might have had. And ... I'm kinda hoping that I'll be there on Thursday. Don't know if I'll manage it though. Could you wake me, just in case?"

"Course I can. What time do you want to be there?"

"I need to be at Jason's flat by nine-thirty. He's going with her and I think she's going to spend the night with him."

"Do you want me to help?"

"Yeah ... that'd be good."

I was there at nine-thirty precisely on Thursday. But Kirsty's body had already gone. I jumped onto a tube then sprinted to Jason's flat. I was just in time. Poppy was getting into Jason's car; Kirsty was in the back seat.

"Come on, Ro," Kirsty said as she saw me. "I'm not getting through to her."

Poppy was by now installed in the front seat, so I had to push my way through her and the seat.

"Euww, I felt something strange." Poppy said.

"What sort of strange?" Jason frowned.

"Like ... I dunno. But, I know this is gonna sound totes mad, but I saw her. Kirsty."

"It's because we were talking about her at the weekend, babes. I felt her presence, that day. But it's wishful thinking, that's all. You'd been looking at her photos."

"If I'd have seen one of those photo images it'd make sense. But she didn't look like that. She was only half-dressed, for one thing."

I swear I could see the colour drain from Jason's face. "What – what was she wearing?"

"A giant T-shirt with a picture of Johnny Depp on it."

Jason grabbed her arm. "Stop shittin' me, Pops. I don't know who told you that's what she was wearing when she died, but it's not funny."

Well, you can imagine how the conversation went after that. "Ssh, let them work it out for themselves," I whispered to Kirsty. By the time Jason and Poppy had settled into a bewildered silence, I nudged Kirsty and said, "You're on."

"Pops, listen to me," Kirsty said.

"I'm listening," Poppy murmured, and mouthed to Jason, "It's her."

"Do you really want to get rid of this baby?"

"N-no, but how can I keep it? I'm only nineteen."

"Looks to me that you've got a family that loves you. And now you've got me watching over you, and I know that we've never met, but I love you, Poppy, and I'll make sure that you cope."

"Stop the car!" Poppy shouted.

And then I disappeared from the scene, and didn't see Kirsty again for two months.

CHAPTER 18

But then there were setbacks.

"It was never going to be plain sailing. Keep at it," said Frank from our familiar bench. Hampstead Heath was gorgeous at this time of year – all reds and golds and showers of leaves.

"I will," I sighed. "There are so many sports clubs at his college; badminton seemed like a good idea. I should have looked myself, checked the standard of the club."

I hung my head, remembering yesterday's awful evening with Oliver.

"Well that was a fucking disaster," he'd said, slamming his racket into the sofa with such force he dented the cushion. "Right bunch of arseholes. My stammer came back, big time. And I was the worst one there."

"I'm sorry, sweetheart. Can't win 'em all, I guess." I knew how patronising I sounded as soon as the words left my mouth, but it was one of those times when nothing I said would be right.

"What are you, my girlfriend or my bloody mother?" Oliver had shouted. "Can't we just have fun, the way we used to?"

Now, sitting with Frank, I remembered the blissful afternoon we'd spent here together last autumn, walking hand in hand, him kicking piles of leaves into the air.

"He was right, too," I said, "We don't have as much fun as we used to. I have most of my laughs with Kirsty these days, when I get to see her, and Oliver's become my project. But the weirdest thing was the way I disappeared immediately after he yelled at me. I guess it was the shock. But when I returned, only a few minutes had passed, and he was slumped in the chair, sobbing his heart out. It was the saddest sight I ever saw, reminded me of when he was a little boy, crying about the school bullies."

"Poor kid." Frank shook his head. "Sounds like most of it's working though."

"Mostly it is. He goes drinking with the lads from college every Friday since term started, and his stammer's improved. He's been to see a couple of concerts with them, and he doesn't spend so much time on those online games. But he's still happiest when it's just me and him. The best bit of the summer was still the three weeks we spent going round the States in a campervan. Those national parks are awesome."

"You said." By now I recognised the expression that meant I'd rambled on about one subject for too long and Frank was bored. "Seems like the two of you are pretty good at seeing the world without being part of it. But you never told me how you got on with the long-haul flight?"

"It was the strangest thing. I disappeared once when Oliver nodded off, but apparently when he woke up he panicked and then I walked down the cabin and sat on his lap, the way I did when we set off."

"You need to slow down a bit. You look knackered. Remember Christine?"

The woman, killed changing a light fitting in her late thirties, appeared to be staying on earth to see her children through to adulthood.

"Yeah, but I haven't seen her for ages. Last time I saw her, she was telling me how worried she was about one of her kids who was taking drugs. What happened?"

"Thought I'd told you. Dave knew her better than most – they used to come here and chat. He said she got weaker and weaker with worry, then about a month ago, passed over right in front of him, no warning. Guess she just plain wore herself out."

What was Frank suggesting, that I might pass over without saying goodbye to Oliver? He wouldn't survive it. I'd have to be more careful.

"You're right, I am doing too much. I wish I saw more of Kirsty."

"Best you let her sleep when she needs it. She's got her

own work to do." Kirsty was now materialising at her parents' house without my help – Poppy had moved back. She'd decided to keep the baby and while no-one was exactly overjoyed about it, they were giving her the support she needed. The downside was that I couldn't always find Kirsty when I wanted to see her.

"Oliver needs to do more exercise. He's putting on weight."

"Think you'd better lighten up on the group things. How about running? I see all shapes and sizes jogging around here, and sometimes they stop and chat to each other. You could go with him at first."

"Frank, you're a genius," I said, impulsively kissing his stubbly cheek and grinning at his the way his face crinkled with pleasure.

And so the following weekend saw Oliver jogging, red-faced and sweaty. He stopped and doubled over, gasping for breath. I stopped beside him, then started running again. Of course for me it was effortless.

"Come on, old man. Keep up."

"Not fair," he said between gritted teeth, but he was smiling.

"OK, let's walk for a while."

At that point I spotted a runner heading towards us. Her face was familiar. Where had I seen her before? Ah yes, it was the girl who'd talked to Oliver last spring when we'd been flying the kite. For a moment, jealousy gripped me; here I was, in my sweater, leggings and slippers, while Judy looked ultra cool in her co-ordinated running gear – all logos and fluorescent stripes. For a moment I thought about changing directions – Oliver hadn't noticed Judy – but no, I mustn't. Social interaction was the whole point of this, wasn't it?

"Look, there's that girl, Judy, remember? You could say hello to her," I said.

"Hi, Judy," he said.

I was pleased to see that, close up, Judy didn't look quite so cool. Her running face was similar to Oliver's, more grim determination than enjoyment, but she recognised him, smiled and removed her headphones. Damn.

"Hi, Oliver, isn't it? You're a runner too?" She even remembered his name.

"That's a bit of an exaggeration, I've just started." Oliver grinned. Judy's eyes darted downwards then back up.

"Say something encouraging to her," I prompted, even though I wanted to slap Judy's face for being so sweet and pretty and ... alive.

"D'you come here often?" Oliver said.

I groaned. "We're going to have to work on your chat-up lines."

But Judy was smiling. "Yeah, I always come here on a Sunday morning. It's my favourite place in the whole of London. You feel you've left the city behind."

Oliver smiled. "I know exactly what you mean. It's one of the few places you can really breathe. Hopefully I'll see you soon."

"Hope so. See you," she said, and carried on running.

"Come on, you've had enough time to rest," I said. I knew that my voice had an edge; I hadn't wanted them to get on that well. We carried on running in silence. It wasn't until we reached the house that either of us spoke.

"I can tell you're upset," Oliver said. "So give up on getting me to talk to girls. Are you trying to get rid of me?"

"Do you know what it does to me to imagine you with someone else? But I've got to be realistic. I don't think I can be with you forever."

"Hey, what's brought this on? Come here; you like me sweaty don't you?"

He held me against him and I drank in great lungfuls of him, but that irresistible masculinity of his scent only reminded me of everything he was and I wasn't. Once home, I watched him shower and dry – we'd progressed to all sorts of touching except going the whole way – and as usual I was left with guilt of how physically frustrating I must be for him. We retreated to our safe cocoon of films and music but I felt as if a cloud had gathered over my head and it wouldn't shift.

That night, I wanted to sleep, but I felt a compulsion to visit the Heath, as if someone else was calling me. Turns out my instinct was right. Frank was sitting on the bench, his head in his hands.

"Hey, what's up?" I said.

"Thank God. I was willing you to show up. I just wanted to say goodbye. It's Jean, y'see. She's gone into hospital. Pneumonia."

"Oh Frank," I said.

"I can't stop; reckon she hasn't got long." He stood up and put his arms around me, and held me for a long time. There was more affection in that hug than I'd ever got from my dad. "I always wanted a daughter of me own. Perhaps we'll see you on the other side."

"I hope so." My voiced wobbled on the last word.

It was the last time I ever saw Frank. Two weeks later, I made my way to the place where I'd met him for the first time. His grave was covered with fresh flowers, and the inscription had changed.

Here lies

Frank MacLean

Died 1985, aged 57 years

Beloved husband and father

And also his wife, Jean

Died 2015, aged 79 years

Reunited at last

I slumped to my knees and sobbed. It had been an unlikely friendship, but one of the most precious of my whole existence. "Goodbye, Frank," I whispered. "Hope they have whisky on the other side."

CHAPTER 19

15th November 2015

"Pete's invited me to go away for Christmas," said Oliver, his voice hesitant. "There's a group of them, going to a cottage in the Peak District."

"That's brilliant. You should go." I tried to sound more enthusiastic than I felt. I'd seen Kirsty earlier that day and she was full of excitement about spending Christmas with her family. Poppy only saw and heard her every now and again, but it was enough to give Kirsty a purpose. It felt as though no-one needed me any more.

"Will you come too?" he asked.

"No, I don't think so." Watching a group of people enjoying roast turkey? That would be more than I could stand. Besides, I was tired like I'd never been, a weary, dreary feeling, as if I was getting old. "You've been doing OK without me, haven't you? Let's face it, I'm pretty useless at Christmas. Can't pull a cracker, can't even get you a present. I wouldn't mind a rest. Me and you can have our own Christmas when you get back."

"What about my stammer? It's always worse when you're not around."

"It's much better than it was. I got Kirsty to eavesdrop on you last week in the uni bar and she said you were transformed."

"You didn't tell me!"

"Course not, that's the point of eavesdropping. Sorry, sweetheart. I had to be sure that you were OK if I wasn't around."

"Why?' That frown again. "Thinking of going somewhere?"

"No but ... y'know. Sometimes I sleep longer than I expect

to. Now you promise me you'll go and have a good time."

"OK, but I'll miss you."

"You started this, remember?" I said to myself. Christmas in a cottage with friends. It was the sort of thing I dreamed of. But my stabs of envy never lasted. Oliver was no longer living on the fringes of life, and it thrilled me. And it would give me a chance to rest. Things were starting to go wrong, you see. My absences were becoming more unpredictable, unsettling both of us.

And so autumn turned to winter, and I spent every day with Oliver, forcing myself to stay present, knowing that I'd sleep for ten days at Christmas. And in all this time, I didn't see Kirsty, not once. It didn't seem fair any more to keep waking her, so we'd agreed to go up to Parliament Hill around midnight if we weren't sleeping. We figured that way, there'd be a good chance of seeing each other. But so far it hadn't happened – I guess it was just too difficult for her now that Poppy was based out in Buckinghamshire with her parents. Sometimes my afterlife was as unfair as my real life had been. I was pleased for Kirsty, but missed her like mad. I missed Frank too – who'd have thought that a drunken old Yorkshireman would come to mean so much to me? I'd met some new people on the Heath – a group of teenagers killed in a house fire – and was showing them the ropes of being a ghost, but it wasn't the same.

When I said goodbye to Oliver, that dark December morning, the sense of loss was sharp and swift, like a knife wound. The end was coming; I was sure of it.

"Hey, are you crying?" he said.

"No, I'm just excited for you. Now, get yourself off and have an amazing time, then come back and relive it all with me."

And then the room started spinning, signalling that it was time for me to leave him.

I woke with a shudder. Where the hell was I? I looked around – no, I'd never been here before. I wouldn't have forgotten somewhere so lovely. The street was dotted with the prettiest stone cottages you ever saw. To one side was a field of grazing sheep, stretching out to snow-covered hills in the distance. And next to me was a barn that had been converted into cottages, the doors of each decorated with wreathes of holly and fir branches. Yellow light glowed from the windows. The scene was perfect; it only needed a sprinkle of glitter and I'd have believed that I'd been transported into a Christmas card.

Then I got it. Some instinct led me to the furthest of the cottages, and I gazed through the window. Inside, eight people were eating Christmas dinner. Pulled crackers were scattered all over the table, which heaved with half-full bowls of roast potatoes, stuffing and vegetables. On a plate stood the remnants of a carved turkey. Everyone had a glass of wine and was wearing a paper hat. And there was Oliver, his face relaxed, chatting away with a man and a woman seated opposite him. I could tell by the movement of his lips that his words were fluent, only a hint of a stumble over a consonant here and there. And I'm proud to say that the pang of jealousy was mild and fleeting. Of course I'd have loved to join him. But that wasn't why I was here; I was sure of it. I was here to see for myself that he could cope without me.

My work was complete.

I turned and walked away, my step heavy. Why was I so exhausted?

And then I woke up in the familiar living room, with that heavy feeling you get when you've had a really good night's sleep after a few bad nights. Oliver was curled in the corner of the sofa, hugging one of the fuchsia cushions against him. His fingers were in his mouth.

"Happy Christmas, sweetheart," I whispered.

He leaped up as if he'd been electrocuted and crushed me against him.

"Wow, that's a hell of a welcome," I said.

"Thank God. Where have you been? I've been back a week," he murmured into my hair.

"Oh no." I pulled away, frowning.

"It's the tenth of January," he muttered.

"Damn. I guess I just needed the rest. I woke up outside the cottage where you spent Christmas, and I saw you, looked like you were having a good time. Then I felt this incredible tiredness and now I'm here."

"You saw me, and you didn't come in?"

"I didn't want to put you off. It looked amazing."

And then he turned from me and put a hand across his face. I placed a hand on his shoulder and felt it shake. I moved to face him and lowered his hand. His face was wet with tears. I wiped them from his face and his tears lingered on my fingers.

"Hey, what is it?"

"I thought that this was it. That you'd passed." His voice was tight.

"Don't cry, I can't stand it."

I cradled his face in my hands, kissed the salt tears away, and didn't speak until his breathing had gone back to normal.

"Come on, I'm dying to know what I missed out on," I said.

"OK, I admit, I had a great time. There were eight of us, and I only knew Pete and Sue. It was the sort of thing that I'd normally have hated. It's exactly the group size I'm uncomfortable with; you know, at dinner everyone's trying to compete with each other to tell a funny story."

I nodded. I felt exactly the same about that sort of group size; I'd prefer to slope off with one person and have a proper conversation.

"But I did it. I joined in, even though I couldn't tell most of my best stories because they involved you. I played drinking games and did tequila slammers." He laughed. "Ended up with a stinking hangover. We went out walking and had lunch in this quirky little pub fifty metres up the road – you'd have loved it. We played board games. But it was exhausting. It all felt a huge effort. And afterwards, I felt guilty for enjoying myself. I should have been with you. I wondered if that's why you hadn't come back. And at New Year, when everyone was kissing everyone else, I kissed all the girls, but it didn't feel right. I wanted to kiss you."

OK, I admit, the thought of him kissing other girls gave me a painful twinge but I ignored it. I looked at him through lowered eyelids and spoke in as coy a voice as I could manage.

"So you didn't enjoy kissing them, even a little bit?"

"There was this one girl, Philippa. I think Sue was trying to fix me up with her. But no, it looks like my heart belongs to you."

And it was up to me to give it away.

CHAPTER 20

17th January 2016

I'd been wandering on the Heath most nights, since I got back, but hardly anyone was out. Even though ghosts didn't feel the cold, it seemed that no-one wanted to be out in the blizzards that January brought.

And still no sign of Kirsty. I'd popped over to Finchley cemetery earlier in the day, but her body wasn't there. So she was around. Poppy must be due to give birth by now, surely.

But I remembered how Frank had summoned me that night. If I focussed with all the effort I could muster, could I transmit a message to Kirsty that I wanted to see her?

I put all my energy into conjuring Kirsty on the bench next to me.

And waited.

And waited.

Oh, it was hopeless. But I had nothing better to do and so carried on sitting there, becoming hypnotised by the swirling of the snowflakes.

I'd lost track of the time when I heard her voice.

"Ro!"

"Kirsty! So it did work! I tried to see if I could make you come here. Took your time, though."

"Well, what did you expect? Poppy had just got little Harry off to sleep when I got this overwhelming feeling that I needed to come here. So I jumped on the last tube and legged it all the way from Finchley Road. What's up?"

"Nothing, I just really wanted to see you. So Poppy's had a baby boy?"

"Yeah, she went into labour on New Year's Eve – that buggered up Jason and Tim's party plans. They went with her to the hospital though, and sat with her through the labour. So

155

did I, and we talked to each other the whole way through. Afterwards, she said, 'Thanks, big sis. Couldn't have done it without you.' Jason and Tim think she's a bit nuts but kind of accept it. Little Harry was 2.3 kilos. He was the first baby born in the hospital in 2016 – made the papers and everything."

"Ah, lovely. How's Poppy coping with being a mum?"

"Complete natural. Funny, no-one wanted her to have it; they all thought she should finish her degree. But she confided in me how badly she'd been doing in college. She'd always struggled with exams and stuff – only did the course because Mum and Dad wanted it. She never felt she was any good at anything, and I was this ideal daughter she could never live up to." She chuckled. "I've put her right on that."

"So you and her have proper conversations now?"

"Yeah. In the last few months, she can see and hear me most of the time. It's been brilliant, getting to know her. Sorry I haven't seen you though. I've been here a couple of times, but I guess we just missed each other. What's new with you?"

"I've got a feeling my time's running out." I sighed. "I can't control my coming and going as well as I used to. And I thought Oliver was ready. He's made more new friends since he got back to college and even had a fantastic Christmas in a cottage with a group of friends. But the strangest thing happened; I showed up outside the cottage and saw him for myself, but only for about five minutes, then I slept for sixteen days. And since then, he's been behaving oddly. Clingy. He can sense I'm slipping away from him and he's resisting it. He had a great time at that cottage; I can tell. They've all become his Facebook friends and posted heaps of photos. He's even out clubbing tonight. But he feels guilty about enjoying himself without me."

"Seems like you're nearly done here," she said.

"Yeah, I think so."

We carried on chatting, and the scariest feeling came over me, that this might be the last time I'd ever see Kirsty. I think she felt it too, because she wouldn't stop. We talked about everything that night – the dreams we hadn't fulfilled, the fun we used to have together, then a nostalgia-fest about our first loves, our favourite music, telly, films, everything. By the end we were talking absolute rubbish, but neither of us wanted the night to end. At some point, it stopped snowing. Then the sky started to lighten and a manic black Labrador bounded up to us, barking furiously, followed by a puzzled man.

"Blimey, the dog walkers have started already," I said. "We must've been here seven hours. Time to go, I guess."

We looked at each other.

I was the first to break the silence.

"Look, Kirsty, I'm not sure when or if we'll see each other again."

"I'm kind of thinking the same. I don't even know if Poppy needs me any more. Maybe I'll pass on or whatever happens. You're about to, I'm sure of it. You even look different tonight. We never got a chance to say goodbye properly first time round, did we? So why don't we do it now?"

We hugged each other, then fell into that awkward silence again. Then we both giggled. Neither of us were any good at being serious with each other.

"Best friends forever," we both whispered at once.

And then came the dizziness.

It turns out I was right. I never did see Kirsty again.

***

Oliver was eating his breakfast when I got back, looking like death.

"God, what happened to you?" I said.

"Hangover from hell," he said.

"So I came straight here." Amazing. I assumed after the night with Kirsty, I might sleep for a week. "How was it?"

"You'd have loved that club, though. It was a retro night – all eighties and nineties stuff. The Cure, the Smiths. Awesome. There's another one next month; you should come. It's too loud to talk in there anyway; you could dance along with us and no-one would know."

"Yeah, maybe I will. Who was there?"

"Just the usual gang: Pete, Sue, Phil, Scott, oh, and a couple of guys on Scott's course."

Already the Christmas friends had become the gang, and

Philippa had become Phil. This was good, this was the way it was meant to be.

All I needed to work out now was how to break it to him that I wouldn't be around much longer. And how, exactly I was going to leave. I was only certain of one thing. I wasn't going without That Kiss.

CHAPTER 21

"You're not going out on the Heath tonight, are you?" Oliver asked.

"No, I'm all yours tonight."

"That's good."

He drew me closer to him, but I could feel his tension. He looked at me suspiciously every time he left the room, expecting me to disappear. I'd become determined to materialise every day, but in the process I seemed to have lost the ability to rest at all. Some nights I didn't even leave the living room.

"I was wondering, would you sleep with me tonight?" he said. "No funny stuff. I just want to feel what it'd be like to sleep with you in my arms."

I thought of a million reasons why this might be a terrible idea but I didn't say them. Things between us were going well, but he still had days where he was moody, touchy, interpreting everything I said as a sign that I didn't love him any more. Besides, if my time was running out, what better way to spend it than lying beside him all night? Or why not go tonight? If only it were that easy.

"That sounds fantastic," I said.

I perched on the end of the bed, waiting for him to emerge from the bathroom, and wondered if sleeping with him would be physically possible. I couldn't even lift the duvet. Eventually he came in. I'd got used to his nakedness, but that aching feeling never became easier to deal with.

"You're not sleeping in that bloody jumper, are you?" He grinned.

I slipped my clothes off, ignoring the catch of his breath. He stepped in the bed and held the duvet for me to join him.

For the first time in almost twenty-one years I lay on a mattress, head on a pillow, a duvet covering me. Oh, it was bliss. Whenever I touched him, it was as if I came back to life. I looked at him and bit my lip. His hand was moving in slow circles on my back. How were we going to avoid any 'funny stuff'?

"If you turn over, we could curl up together, like spoons," he suggested.

I turned over and he placed an arm around me, resting under my boobs. I let out a deep sigh.

"This is amazing," I murmured.

But how I'd ever sleep was another thing. And he obviously felt the same. His arm didn't stay still and soon I'd turned around to face him and he was kissing my neck. Then he pushed me away.

"Let's not push our luck," he mumbled.

I willed myself not to sleep, in case I didn't wake here, in the bed. Or maybe I would? Maybe this would be the thing that restored my life. It was such a delicious fantasy that my body relaxed, and when I woke it was to the sound of Oliver shouting my name. But we weren't in bed. For one thing, I was surrounded by grass. I rubbed my eyes – why couldn't I focus?

"Rowena, wake up."

Ah, now I could feel his grip on my shoulders. I screwed up my eyes tightly and reopened them. That was better, I could see. We were in a graveyard.

"Oliver, where are we?"

But before he had time to answer, I'd worked it out. I was on the patch of grass by my gravestone. I must have gone for a sleep, the way Kirsty did, and Oliver had come to find me. Then I looked at his face – he seemed to have aged. Surely not?

"Hey, you look awful. Have I been gone a while? Is that why you came to find me?"

"Twelve days. I was terrified. I took a day off college and drove up here this morning."

Phew. From the look of his face I wondered if I might have been here a few years. "Oh hell. Last thing I remember was lying in your arms, in bed. It was blissful. Why can't I control this any more? I always used to come back when Marjorie needed me."

"I needed you." His voice was sulky.

"Are you sure?" I said as he helped me to my feet. "Maybe it's a sign that you don't need me so much. You said yourself how your confidence has grown."

"No. I mean, yeah, I admit it. For the first time, I've got a life and it's not all about you. I love the new gang. I'm joining in more at college. That new running club's brilliant. But life's still better with you and I hate going back to an empty house. I mean, if this all means you're going to disappear for weeks on end, I'd rather have things the way they were."

"But maybe we have no choice. You've noticed I'm getting more tired. I don't think I'll be able to go skiing."

"Oh no. I'll cash in my ticket."

"You could go alone. Or see if one of the gang wants to go?"

"How could I, remembering how it was last year, with you?"

"I think we've got to face facts, Oliver." My voice lowered. "My time's coming."

"But how can it be?"

"I don't know. I feel that maybe … ghosts only have so much energy, like a battery that's running down. The reason I lasted nineteen years was because I had far more sleeping time than waking. And now I'm running out of power. If I'm going to carry on being with you, I'm going to need more down time, and that's not going to be enough for you, is it? I need to set you free."

"But you're the love of my life. How can I go on, knowing that anyone else I meet could only ever be second best?"

"You will, because that's what people do. Oh, don't look at me like that." And then a gigantic wave of self-pity washed over me. "Do you think I want it this way? I'm the one who's dead, remember. Don't you think I'd give anything to be a living being again? To be able to kiss someone and spend time with them and not end up asleep in a graveyard? To get married and have children and grow old with someone? The two years we've had have been incredible. I've been happy in a way I never believed possible. But I think we've cheated fate for too long, don't you?"

"I'm just so bloody scared. Scared that one day I'll come home and you're gone forever."

"So let's do it properly. Kiss me."

"I'm not ready to."

We hardly spoke on the drive home. I didn't even make it back. As we pulled off the motorway, I felt that familiar dizziness and the next thing I knew, I was back on the sofa. I found Oliver in the kitchen, stirring a pan of soup.

"Hi. What day is it?" I said.

When he turned, I noticed that dark circles had carved themselves under his eyes. His hair was uncombed and his T-shirt full of stains. I gave him a hug and wrinkled my nose. Had he even washed today?

"Saturday. Three days after I last saw you. Half the weekend gone." His voice was heavy with accusation

"Oh no. I'm sorry. But you went out last night, didn't you?"

"No, I ducked out. Didn't feel like seeing anyone. You see, I've been thinking. There's another option, for both of us, to be together, but I couldn't do it until you were here." He walked over to the sink and, taking a glass from the draining board, filled it with water. Moving to the drawers, he took out a small plastic container. "Paracetamol. 24 should do it."

He opened the bottle and emptied a few pills into his cupped hand.

"No!" I darted forward and grabbed his hands, forcing him to drop the pills.

"Why not? We'd be together forever."

"Because it won't work. Remember Alice? Her soul split into a million tiny fragments. If you did that, we'd definitely never see each other again. You can't cheat death. You can only come with me when it's your time. But Oliver, whatever happens, we're soul mates. We'll find each other again in the next life. Let's just enjoy what time we have left."

He slumped to the floor. I knelt beside him, cradling her head against him. This is how it would be from now on, wouldn't it? Floundering in a growing unease until I faded away. It was time for me to take control. He might resist, but this time, my determination would make me see it through. Not yet, his birthday was coming up. But I couldn't keep saying this forever; there'd always be excuses to put it off. And then I had it. I'd go on Marjorie's anniversary – March 29th. Exactly two years together. That would give us one last month to treasure.

CHAPTER 22

14th February 2016

When I woke up on the sofa, it was still dark on the outside. I looked at the computer – Oliver always kept it on for me and disabled the screensaver so I could keep track of time. 6:30 am, Sunday the 14th. Thank God. I'd spent the remainder of the Saturday with him and had willed every cell of my body to turn up today. Pity I couldn't buy him a Valentine's card, like a normal person.

He thundered downstairs, the way he always did these days, and let out a huge breath when he saw me.

"Thank God, I so wanted you to be here today. Happy Valentine's day, gorgeous. I know you can't open it, but here's your card."

He opened the card in front of me, a cute-but-funny one and exactly what I'd have chosen for him.

"How do you fancy champagne for breakfast?" he said.

I can still feel those bubbles bursting against my lips. We had them again, for Oliver's birthday, March 6th, the twenty-first anniversary of my death. We spent the weekend in Suffolk, and Oliver put flowers on my grave. I resisted the temptation to gatecrash his party though. Judging by the state of him the next day, it was a good one.

I could write a whole book on those last weeks. We seemed to cram a lifetime's worth of memories into them, each sweeter by no longer having the uncertainty of what would happen in the future. And I'm sure Oliver knew and finally accepted it too. But endless details of good times are tedious for the listener, aren't they? You only want to hear about the drama and conflict. So all I'll say is that, if there's a heaven on the other side, it can't possibly be as good as those times with Oliver.

And so here I am, back where I started. My last night on earth. If everything goes to plan.

***

29th March 2016.

I couldn't be late, could I? I'm here, in the kitchen, right on cue, at eight o'clock in the morning. My new resolve to control my passing seems to have improved my ability to control my presence.

I feel like Oliver and I have lived a lifetime together in the last two years. The early weeks were a happy childhood and adolescence combined. In teaching Oliver to deal with the world of social interactions and all its complications, we both matured. The last six weeks have been my autumn years. Next to the Valentine's card and birthday cards (I'd insisted on him not taking them down – he'd need something to cheer him up after I'd gone) lay Oliver's medal – a 10K race. I'd stood at the finish line, bursting with pride. Now's definitely the right time.

"Hope you're going to be there to show me the ropes, Marjorie," I whisper to the photo on the mantelpiece.

I'm still lost in happy reminiscences when I hear Oliver's footsteps. He stands behind me and places a hand on my shoulder.

"I can't believe it's been two years."

I turn to face him and take his hands. I gaze into those delicious blue eyes, hoping he'll grasp the intention behind mine. No point in putting it off. It has to be now, or I'll lose my nerve.

"It's been the happiest two years of my life." My words are slow and deliberate.

He tightens his grip on my hand. The pressure's painful – funny, I've forgotten what physical pain felt like.

"Me too," he says. And I can see that he gets it. And he's ready.

But I'm not giving him a chance to become maudlin. I guess you know me well enough by now to realise that I've planned this moment to the last detail – my romantic swansong.

"Can you put some music on?" I say. "Paul Weller – *You do something to me.* I feel like dancing"

He picks up his iPad, selects the track, and the room is filled with the song that started our enchanted relationship. We sway in each other's arms until the music fades away. His hands fan over my cheeks and linger, framing my face. I stand on tiptoe to bring my mouth towards his. His breath mingles with mine, warm and sweet.

"I knew you were going to choose today." His voice is unsteady.

"It's time, Oliver. I'm setting you free. But promise me that you'll get out there, meet someone else. You can do it now."

"How can I love anyone the way I love you? We're twin souls, remember."

"We have lots of lives to live; I'm certain of it. We won't find each other every time. But I'll wait for you. We'll be together in the next one."

He opens his mouth to protest but I place a finger to his lips, and then press my lips to his. At first they're hard, unyielding, like before, but I increase the pressure and his mouth gradually softens and moulds to mine. And now we can't stop, gorging on the taste of each other. This is incredible! Nothing exists except the two of us.

When we pull apart, neither of us state the obvious. Have I got it wrong, or is God, if there is one, giving me a break for once and letting me have it all? Oliver's not stopping to ask. He takes my hand and leads me to the bedroom. And finally, we discover each other completely. And no, I'm not spilling the details, except to say wow. Oh wow.

And I'm still here, my head rising and falling on the wave of his breathing. But now something's happening, an ecstatic rush, just when I thought I couldn't feel anything better than what's just happened.

"Rowena, this is incredible …"

Oliver's voice shakes me. I've been so lost in the intensity of my emotions that I haven't noticed that I'm losing my physicality.

So this is it.

But I'm not disappearing. Huh? I'm sinking into Oliver's body, merging with him. I turn my head in time to take one last look at his face. Oh good, he's not frightened. He looks so beautiful, so joyful. I open my mouth to say goodbye but no words are coming out. But of course, I don't need to say goodbye. I've found my final resting place. This is my chance to make an impact on the world. I'll live on, through him.

The light's fading and ...

CHAPTER 23
OLIVER

22nd June 2016

I like to get to Parliament Hill early on a Sunday morning, to make sure my bench is free. Today looks set to be a busy one – we've had the best heatwave ever for the last few weeks – though the morning feels a bit fresher, a light breeze causing a ripple among the leaves on the trees. The first of the kite flyers has arrived. I must get mine out again. I smile, sit down and close my eyes, and soon I'm lost in happy memories.

I'm interrupted by a vaguely familiar voice.

"Oliver, hi. I haven't seen you for ages."

I squint and look up. Oh, it's that girl, Judy. She's got a dusting of freckles across her nose, just like mine. Cute. Say something encouraging. I love the way I can immediately conjure up Rowena's voice inside my head.

"Hi Judy, good to see you." I smile and glance to the sky with gratitude. My stammer seems to have gone for good. "No, I haven't been out for a while. I've been through a bit of a rough patch."

That's putting it mildly. Those early days were the worst of my life; when I missed Rowena so much that I had to remind myself to get out of bed every morning, to dress and to eat breakfast. The house felt so wrong without her; she'd been as much a part of it as the walls and the ceiling. But soon I realised that she'd stayed with me. When I went back to college, it was all less of an effort than usual. I didn't need to act confident any more. Rowena's personality seemed to have somehow melded with mine, and with it all the lessons she'd learned about life. Don't ask me how, but everything's so much easier now. I've flown through the round of job interviews and have just chosen one of three good offers.

"Sorry to hear that, would it help to talk about it?" Judy's looking good, better than I remembered.

"A friend died in March. A good friend. But I won't bore you with the details; things are looking up. I've just finished my finals," I said.

"Have you got a job yet?"

"Yeah, I start on a graduate training scheme in September. But before that I'm going inter-railing, with a few friends. Have to make the most of my last summer of freedom."

"How lovely … I'd love to do that." She had this habit of flicking her eyes down and then upwards again; it's kinda sweet.

"Are you a student?" It occurs to me that I don't know anything about her.

"Yes, just finished my second year at Kings."

She sits next to me, we chat for a while, and it's good. She's funny and sweet and self-deprecating all at the same time. Rowena approves of her; I can tell.

"Not flying your kite today?" she says.

"No, funnily enough I was just thinking about that." I look down and bite my lip. Every now and again it hits me like this, the searing pain almost too much to bear. Pull it together, Oliver.

"Maybe I could help sometime," Judy's hesitant.

You're right, Rowena. She's just as unsure of herself as I used to be. I take a deep breath and straighten my shoulders. "That'd be great. Do you fancy a coffee?"

"I'd love one," she says.

As we stand up, Judy glances at the inscription on the bench.

"Have you noticed that this is a new bench? I love reading the inscriptions," she says. "This one's especially sad – look, the girl was the same age as me."

"Yeah, I w-wonder what happened to her?" I swallow.

"And look at the dates. I wonder why it's taken so long for someone to put it here?"

"If someone still remembers her, she must have been special."

We read the small brass plaque:

> ROWENA HILL
>
> 1975-1995
>
> Finally resting in peace
>
> What we have once enjoyed we can never lose;
>
> All that we love deeply, becomes a part of us.

And then we walk down the hill together.

THE BEGINNING

EPILOGUE

June 2108

The girl smiles at the sight of so many people flying at the top of Parliament Hill, their bright KiteSuits bobbing in the breeze. Then she frowns on seeing someone sitting at her bench. But on approaching, she catches her breath. It's a guy, and he's hot. And although there are plenty of spare benches, and she's never done anything so daring in her life, she walks right up to him.

"Do you mind if I sit here?" she says.

He looks up, frowns, stares at her like he knows her but can't place her, and then smiles. Oh, he's got beautiful blue eyes. "No, go ahead. Have we met before?"

"I don't think so." She twists a strand of hair around her finger; it's a silly habit she has when she's nervous, which she is now. Veez, what was she thinking? But the guy's giving her an encouraging smile, so she continues. "I've just moved here. I first saw this bench a few weeks ago – I love the old wooden ones – and the inscription got to me. The girl was the same age as me, you see."

"Funny, I'm drawn to this bench too. I like her name. Ro-wee-na." He says the word slowly and deliberately, emphasising every syllable. "She must have been special. But there's another reason I come here. My great-grandfather dedicated this bench; my Mum found the paperwork after he died."

"Paperwork?" The expression isn't familiar.

"Everything was recorded on paper in those days; hard to imagine, isn't it?" he says.

"So how did he know Rowena?" Please let it be a romantic story; she's addicted to RomMovies.

"We have no idea. The invoice was dated 2016, twenty-one

years after she died. And she died the year he was born, so he can't have known her."

"Oh, I'm disappointed. And your great-grandfather never mentioned the name?"

"Not as far as my Mum knows. I never met him; he died a couple of days before I was born. But I've always felt I knew him, perhaps because he's quite famous." He holds up the DataBand on his wrist and smiles. "He invented the virtual screen and quite a few other things."

"Woow. Oliver Spencer was your great-grandfather? I wrote an essay on him for my finals." This boy's eyes are having a disconcerting effect on her. "But it makes the story of Rowena even more fascinating. I'd imagined her grief-stricken lover put the inscription here."

"Yeah ... I hope she found love before she died." He holds his DataBand towards hers to exchange details. "Let's connect."

But she has the strangest feeling that they already have.

Acknowledgements

Thanks to my husband, Gerry, for your constant love, patience and support. None of this would be possible without you. Thanks, Mam, Alex and Steve for always believing in me and being there when I need you.

I'm grateful to all my friends; not only for your encouragement but also for your company. Writing can be a solitary occupation and it's good to know you're out there. Thanks to Diana McGarry for your advice, critiques and proofreading.

Special thanks go to Peter and Alison Buck and the rest of the Elsewhen team for their guidance during the editing and publishing process. I feel proud and privileged to be published by such an enthusiastic and supportive company.

Finally, thanks for reading this. I'm grateful to everyone who reviewed my previous novels, either on Amazon, Goodreads or book blogs. Reviews greatly increase the book's visibility and create sales. If you've enjoyed this one, please consider leaving a review; every one counts!

Elsewhen Press

an independent publisher specialising in Speculative Fiction

Visit the Elsewhen Press website at elsewhen.press for the latest
information on all of our titles, authors and events; to read our blog; find
out where to buy our books and ebooks; or to place an order.

Sign up for the Elsewhen Press InFlight Newsletter at
elsewhen.press/newsletter

THE BLUEPRINT TRILOGY
KATRINA MOUNTFORT

The *Blueprint* trilogy takes us to a future in which men and women are almost identical, and personal relationships are forbidden. Following a bio-terrorist attack, the population now lives within comfortable Citidomes. MindValues advocate acceptance and non-attachment. The BodyPerfect cult encourages a tall thin androgynous appearance, and looks are everything.

In *Future Perfect* we are introduced to Caia, an intelligent and highly educated young woman. In spite of severe governmental and societal strictures, Caia finds herself attracted to her co-worker, Mac, a rebel whose questioning of their so-called utopian society both adds to his allure and encourages her own questioning of the status quo. As Mac introduces her to illegal and subversive information she is drawn into a forbidden, dangerous world, alienated from her other co-workers and the companions with whom she shares her residence. In a society where every thought and action is controlled, informers are everywhere; whom can she trust? Katrina's story examines the enforcement of conformity through fear, the fostering of distorted and damaging attitudes towards forbidden love, manipulation of appearance and even the definition of beauty.

In *Forbidden Alliance* we return to Caia and Mac some sixteen years later in a story that poses questions of leadership, family loyalties and whether it is possible to justify the sacrifice of human lives for the greater good.

In *Freedom's Prisoners* tensions have escalated. The rebels may have won the first battle in their fight against the Citidome authorities, but can they win a war? The Citidomes are fighting back and no-one is safe any more as RotorFighters rain down fire on defenceless villages destroying them and their inhabitants. Katrina explores betrayal, guilt, hope and endurance in an explosive conclusion to the *Blueprint* trilogy.

The *Blueprint* trilogy is a thought-provoking series with a dark undercurrent that will appeal to both an adult and young adult audience.

Book 1: *Future Perfect*
ISBN: 9781908168559 (epub, kindle) / 9781908168450 (288pp paperback)

Book 2: *Forbidden Alliance*
ISBN: 9781908168900 (epub, kindle) / 9781908168801 (288pp paperback)

Book 3: *Freedom's Prisoners*
ISBN: 9781911409120 (epub, kindle) / 9781911409021 (288pp paperback)

Visit bit.ly/BlueprintTrilogy

LiGa series

Sanem Ozdural

A thought-provoking series of books in an essentially contemporary setting, with elements of both science fiction and fantasy.

LiGa™

Book I

Literary science fiction, LiGa™ tells of a game in which the players are, literally, gambling with their lives. In the near-future a secretive organisation has developed technology to transfer the regenerative power of a body's cells from one person to another, conferring extended or even indefinite life expectancy. As a means of controlling who benefits from the technology, access is obtained by winning a tournament of chess or bridge to which only a select few are invited. At its core, the game is a test of a person's integrity, ability and resilience. Sanem's novel provides a fascinating insight into the motivation both of those characters who win and thus have the possibility of virtual immortality and of those who will effectively lose some of their life expectancy.

ISBN: 9781908168160 (epub, kindle) / ISBN: 9781908168061 (400pp paperback)

Visit bit.ly/BookLiGa

THE **DARK** SHALL DO WHAT LIGHT CANNOT

Book II

We find out more about the organisation behind LiGa as we travel with some of them to Pera, a place which lies beyond the Light Veil on the other side of reality. There are light trees there that eat sunlight and bear fruit that, in turn, lights up and energises (literally) the community of Pera. There are light birds that glitter in the night because they have eaten the seed of the lightberry. The House of Light and Dark, which is the domain of the Sun and her brother, Twilight, welcomes all creatures living in Pera. But in the midst of all the glitter, laughter and the songs, it must be remembered that the lightberry is poisonous to the non-Pera born, and the Land is afraid when the Sun retreats, for it is then that Twilight walks the streets…

ISBN: 9781908168740 (epub, kindle) / ISBN: 9781908168641 (480pp paperback)

Visit bit.ly/Darkshalldo

SmartYellow™
J.A. Christy

SmartYellow™ is the story of a young girl, Katrina Williams, who finds herself on the wrong side of social services. After becoming pregnant with only a slight notion of the father's identity, she is disowned by her parents and goes to live on a social housing estate. Before long she is being bullied by a gang involved in criminal activity and anti-social behaviour. Seeking help from the authorities she is persuaded to return to the estate to work as part of Operation Schrödinger, alongside a surveillance specialist. But she soon realises that Operation Schrödinger is not what it seems.

Exploring themes of social inequity and scientific responsibility, J.A. Christy's first speculative fiction novel leads her heroine Katrina to understand how probability, hope and empathy play a huge part in the flow of life and are absent in the stagnation of mere survival. As readers we also start to question how we would know if the power of the State to support and care for the weak had become corrupted into the oppression of all those who do not fit society's norms.

SmartYellow™ offers a worryingly plausible and chilling glimpse into an alternate Britain. For the sake of order and for the benefit of more fortunate members of society, those seen as socially undesirable are marked with SmartYellow™, making it easier for them to be controlled and maintained in a state of fruitless inactivity. Writer, J.A. Christy, turns an understanding and honest eye not only onto the weak, who have failed to cope with life, but also onto those who ruthlessly exploit them for their own ends. At times tense and threatening, at times tender and insightful, *SmartYellow*™ is a rewarding and thought-provoking read.

J.A. Christy's writing career began in infant school at the age of seven when she won best poetry prize with her poem '*Winter*'. Since then she has been writing short stories and has had several published in magazines and anthologies.

She holds a PhD in which she explores the stories we use in everyday life to construct our identities. Working in high hazard safety, she is a Chartered Psychologist and Scientist and writes to apply her knowledge to cross the boundaries between science and art, in particular in the crime, speculative and science-fiction genres.

She lives in Oldham with her partner and their dog.

ISBN: 9781908168788 (epub, kindle) ISBN: 9781908168689 (320pp paperback)

Visit bit.ly/SmartYellow

About the author

Katrina Mountfort was born in Leeds. After a degree in Biochemistry and a PhD in Food Science, she started work as a scientist. Since then, she's had a varied career. Her philosophy of life is that we only regret the things we don't try, and she's been a homeopath, performed forensic science research and currently works as a freelance medical writer. She now lives in York with her husband and two dogs. When she hit forty, she decided it was time to fulfil her childhood dream of writing a novel. Her debut novel, *Future Perfect,* the first book in the *Blueprint* trilogy, was published by Elsewhen Press in 2014, followed over the next two years by the rest of the trilogy, *Forbidden Alliance* and *Freedom's Prisoners*. Now Katrina returns to Elsewhen Press with *The Ghost in You*.